A Butterfly Landed On My Face

Arvy Bala

WRITERS' READERS
AN IMPRINT OF BOOKSTHAKAM

Published by Booksthakam, India
info@booksthakam.com
www.booksthakam.com
A Butterfly Landed On My Face
A Booksthakam Book/ published by arrangement with the author

ISBN: 978-93-94378-39-1
Typeset and Cover Design by Cogitabund LLP
Printed and bounded in India by Manipal Technologies Limited
FSC www.fsc.org MIX Paper | Supporting responsible forestry FSC® C043100

Letter to the Reader

Dear Reader,

Firstly, it's my pleasure to present this book to you as a part of your reading experience. Your appreciation encourages me to write even more.

As I sit down to write this foreword, I am ecstatic and filled with a profound sense of gratitude and anticipation. Writing this story has been a journey through months. I am so eager to share with you a wonderful and personal experience. With great excitement and modesty, I invite you into the world I have created – the one I have shaped with countless hours of personal experience, wishes, scars, introspection, invaluable contributions, and a lot more. The story is also indebted to many individuals, who have been a great source of inspiration in my life's journey.

Throughout the process, I have been attracted by the resilience and beauty of nature and the adaptability of human beings. The characters you will meet within this book are a proof of that spirit, each one a reflection of the numerous experiences and emotions that define our existence. They are flawed, yet hopeful; broken, yet resilient. I am hopeful that their stories will resonate with you and that you may find pieces of yourself in their triumphs and struggles.

This book would not have been possible without the unwavering support of my mom who always pushed me to explore new genres, my loved ones, best friends, well-wishing colleagues, and a few more including that one orange cat around my house. They have been my rock and my sounding board. Their encouragement has been a constant source of strength, and for that, I am grateful. I must also extend my heartfelt thanks to Ashvin from Booksthakam whose insights and gentle guidance have helped me throughout this journey to publish my first book.

As you embark on this journey with me, I encourage you to approach it with an open heart and an open mind. The characters and incidents portrayed in this book are a work of fiction and entirely imaginary. Not to be inferred as in the real world, which is much more dramatic, I'd say.

Thank you again, for choosing to spend your time with this story. It is a privilege to share it with you, and I am honored to have you as a reader.

With Love and Peace,

Arvy Bala

A Butterfly Landed On My Face

Hi!

My name is Gautham and this story is me reflecting on the twists and turns that have woven my life together. My story is entangled with threads of love and longing, triumph and suffering, and above all, the relentless pursuit of a heart's desire. Mistakes and experiences have made me a better person.

And hey! Amidst the trials and misfortunes of youth, there was a beacon of light in my path—the promise of love. It was a love that dared to defy the boundaries imposed by circumstance and fate. And amid chaos and confusion, she stood by me, holding my hands, while we grew together into the people we are now.

AN IMPORTANT NOTE! There are a few areas in my story from a third-person perspective and they serve as a creative way of adding drama.

My name is Gautham! This is my story portraying interesting individuals who created a greater impact at the greatest points in my life.

Forgive me, for I have loved...

...the life as it happened. And,

Welcome to my world!

A Butterfly Landed on My Face

Episode #1

ONE at a time

I was quite hungover due to an afternoon nap and skipping to cook lunch, I had already taken off to the mall. As I listened to the songs that were mildly playing on the AirPods, I pictured myself as the protagonist of a movie.

Since it had been a while since I went to the Taco Bell, I walked straight to its counter. Even though I was hesitant, I wanted to order something new from the menu.

'Can I get uh, Cheesy double-decker Taco and a Sriracha Burrito? With a Pepsi black?'

The person at the counter took my number and said, "Sir! You have been our regular customer and have currently accumulated 18,000 points. Do you wish to redeem with any eligible order?"

Not bothering about the judgy looks of the person standing beside me, I declined the offer.

I paid for the order and waited until the order number flashed on the monitor that hung by the sign. When a song was finished from the playlist I was listening to, my order was ready. Picking up the tray and carefully walking through the crowd, I tried my best not to trip over the nicely polished flat floor. Perks of living a clumsy life!

They seemed to have misunderstood my order and thought it was a meal package but I was happy to get the fries too. After looking around for a while, I found a nice round table and sat on it. The songs were still playing. Now I switched to a slower playlist and started to eat the taco. I tried my best not to look like a goat eating a big cabbage leaf. Devouring the taco, I sipped the drink and took off the AirPods. Before opening the wrapper of the burrito, I felt the cover with my hands and found that it was still warm. This was my favourite among all the other items.

Many people were eating in that large food court. Families, kids, crying kids, people on dates, people who were eating peacefully leaving their kids back at home and so on. And many people solo-ing out like our protagonist. I meant, me!

The small and cute round table next to me had no chairs. A woman walked past me and kept the tray on the table. She then came towards me with a smile and asked pointing towards the chair opposite me, 'Is this occupied?'

I asked without hesitation, 'No, if it's okay for you, you can sit here,' and chuckled nervously. Only then did I realize what she said. Ah! Such a ding-dong.

She paused for a moment and lifted the chair. Then she realized what I had spoken. She asked, 'Wait, did you just ask me to sit here?' for which I nervously shook my head. My heart began to race fearing how she was going to react. Looking at my blushing face briefly, she smiled widely again, dropped the chair, and went back to get her food tray. I waited patiently for her to come to the table and sit with me.

'How do you know I came alone?' she asked.

I grinned - 'Lucky guess!' and she smiled.

I then chuckled and continued to say, 'Yeah! If not alone I would have been having a weird conversation with some random person.'

She laughed. 'Not so random anymore, uh?'

'I'm Gautham!'

She lent her left hand to fist bump, 'Sundhari!'

'I'm from Coimbatore.'

'Nice! So, a tamil guy. I can speak well, and read also, but it takes time for me to even read one sentence. I have been here since birth. Both my parents are from here as well. My dad loves watching Tamil films and so we had a chance to watch them too and I learnt most of my Tamil through movies. So, I guess you can do the math.'

'Yeah, yeah! I get that.'

She had ordered pasta from a nearby shop that specialized in pizza. I asked her if she had tried their pizzas. Her answer was quite fascinating because she usually ordered the same pasta everywhere she went. As we continued talking, I came to know that she was finishing up her PhD work while she was holding an offer from a software company for a research position again.

I told her about some funny anecdotes from the office and my love for beaches and travelling; especially I could not shut up about travel. Sundhari, on the other hand, was a researcher and a Software Developer too. She told me about her creative projects and how she enjoyed going back to the office after finishing her research degree. We discovered a shared interest in travelling, and she revealed that she loved taking photos during her adventure-filled trips.

Enjoying the meal, the two strangers found themselves engrossed in conversation, discussing their favourite books, movies, and hobbies. We also spoke about our families and about growing up back in home. The initial awkwardness of being strangers had melted away quickly and soon we felt a genuine connection. I felt quite surprised as I had never spoken so much in such a situation. I opened up about how, some years ago, I had a blind date with someone who was basically a genie giving me company on a solo dinner at a fancy restaurant. She made fun of me as she said, 'OOO! So you have so many fans, huh?' and laughed.

She wanted to give me her number and asked for my number as well. As I pulled out my phone for reasons unknown, she said, 'Dude! I have a 13 mini too!' and showed her iPhone. 'This is such a nice phone. I can never think of another sleek one like it. Fits in the palm and works like a charm.'

Agreeing to what she said, I gave my number. She interrupted, 'Let's try this new feature. I have not tried it since the OS update. She switched on the Airdrop in our phones and tapped their heads together. With a nice animation both our contacts were saved in each other's phones. I said, 'Nice pic!'

She replied with a mischievous smile, 'Oh really? You should see my phone number!'

Going nuts with that reference - 'Did you just quote FRIENDS?'

'Yeah, I'm Princess Consuela. But seriously look at my phone number.'

I saved her contact, peeked at the phone number and saw that it ended with 69. Laughing softly I said, 'Nice!'

After a satisfying lunch and great conversation, we promised each other to keep in touch and perhaps meet again in the future. The chance encounter had turned into a heartwarming experience, reminding them both that meaningful connections could happen when you least expected them.

3 hours later at home

The chatbox is empty. Both of us hesitatingly sent each other a message at the same time,

S - Hey!

G - Hey Gautham here!

S - Oh my god...! I thought someone else :P

G - Yeah, a creep from lunch.

S - Eyy no! A nice-looking chap for sure!

G - Erm?! Thanks, and same to you too :D

S - Yeah, you are welcome, LOL :P

S - Ok, let's talk soon. I'm going out with friends now.

G - Yass! Sure. BTW I had such a nice time in a long time. Thanks, Sundhari!

S - Don't thank me. Buy me an ice cream instead...C yaa ;)

Episode #2

SECOND Chances

'Gautham, if I have to be honest... I am kinda sick today.' Sundhari looked down when I asked her why she was looking dull, even on a hot summer day in the month of March.

She was wearing a mustard yellow sweatshirt complementing her jeans and Converse shoes. Her French braided hair and the way she tied her shoelaces also complemented each other.

I exhaled and then smiled. Her eyes were so tired and she said that she had to catch a cab as she was too exhausted to ride her bike.

'I can see it, Sundhari. You really have to go to a hospital now rather than the cafe.'

Sundhari frowned a bit, winked, and said, 'Okay! But maybe afterwards, when I go home.'

Thinking for a few moments, I felt that it would not be right if I was going to ignore her condition and we started talking about random things. Then I said, 'You know what! I can suggest something. Maybe I can accompany you to the hospital. I promised to pay for the first date but let's do something different. Let's get you alright first. Would that be okay, Sundhari?'

'Yes, Gautham. That will be alright. Tomorrow is Monday but I have already applied for sick leave and informed my Team lead. Now, thank you for asking me to go to the hospital.'

I said, 'Yeah! Of course. Look, I know about your expertise in Python or whatever code language. But you have also talked about your amazing colleagues. They will handle it and it's not like your software is going to break down internationally and cause the internet to shut down globally. And I remember your next update release is only next month! So, health first.'

At the hospital

We did not wait very long at the hospital to find out it was just some mild fever. As we waited for her blood results, I remembered it was Women's Day. So I thought of asking her something.

'Sundhari! Would it be okay, if I can suggest getting you a...full health checkup? It's uh...' clearing my throat and I continued, 'Women's Day. So, I saw some 30% off or something, and if your health insurance is accepted at this hospital, it would be great, right? I mean it's a pretty big joint. I am sure they do.'

'No Gautham. That's kinda expensive and they don't cover liver function tests and all. We still have to pay like two or three thousand even if it is covered.'

I smirked and said, 'And how much do you think we might have spent outside? And hey, I swore to pay for today. Given the discount, I am sure it wouldn't be that much. I'll stay back with you. I mean it's a nice-looking hospital. So, I wouldn't mind spending time with you here.'

A nurse who walked by laughed and said, 'Thank you, sir!'

'You got me on the technicality, my friend!'

'Is that a yes, Ms. Sundhari?'

She smacked her lips and it made a sound which almost resembled that of kissing. She nodded and I went to the reception on the same floor at the end of the hall, to enquire about the full health checkup. Well, our first date ended up at a hospital, she was sick, and also going to take a full health checkup.

Within the next 2 hours, many kinds of tests were done and it was almost past lunchtime. She said she did not feel so hungry while I could have devoured an entire pot of biriyani. But being with her made me feel so content that I actually ignored my hunger. I bought two cans of cold coffee at the canteen and brought them to her who was waiting outside the scan room. I had been trying to entertain her, cracking lame jokes, mostly dad jokes.

'Dude, I cannot have any fluids. The nurse told you, remember?' she asked me, carrying one can of cold coffee in her hand almost ready to throw it at my face. 'But I appreciate the gesture.'

'Ah, thank god. I thought you'd get angry and throw it at my face. '

She sarcastically said, "I kinda wanna try. Never done that before. Well, there's a first time for everything!" We laughed and our laughter echoed in the whole corridor.

I can never forget this date of ours even if I get Alzheimer's. Because what happened after the hospital visit was much more beautiful.

Some months before NOW

I was standing on the balcony and staring at the beach that was visible from afar. We live on the 12th floor and the view is quite stunning. It was a bit chilly that day and was about to rain. The clouds were dark as a blackboard and I could see occasional lightning accompanied by deafening thunders.

It started drizzling and since I was standing near the grill, some raindrops fell on my face.

I could hear her walking from the hall to the balcony. As I wiped off the tears from my face and smiled at her, she came and stood beside me. 'Baby! You don't have to pretend. I see your struggles every single day. You have to take your therapist's advice. It's gonna be fine. It's not something wrong. Maybe only for the diagnosis. Also, since the doctor is in Bangalore, a road trip might also help you.'

'Yes, Sundhari! But what if the doctor...'

'Gautham! The doctor would only understand you, diagnose you and treat you. He's not going to judge who you are. It's a journey da! Remember how you always say, it is not the path that matters but the destination. It is going to get better when we plan our random trips. You have to understand that applies to life too. You can do this!'

'What if I don't become the person I was, Sundhari?'

'Gautham, this is not about becoming who you were. Maybe after all this gets sorted, you will be a new person. More evolved and better than now. Breathe life into that person. That's what healing is all about.'

Words got stuck in my throat and I couldn't speak. My eyes pooled up and I immediately sat down on the floor crying hard. My body was shivering like crazy too. Sundhari sat down right next to me and hugged me. My crying was getting louder. The rain was getting heavier. I was afraid she might get drenched in the rain. Sometimes, she might even get a mild fever. But I couldn't move. I held her right hand and continued crying.

With a crying and a babyish voice I told her, 'I am sorry. I don't know why I am crying.'

Sundhari — 'Shh shh shh shh! You don't have to explain, my love. Just express whatever you are feeling. I am here!'

I looked at her face. The tears had distorted my vision and the heavy raindrops didn't allow me to open my eyes properly. 'Sundhari! What if I lose myself? Maybe the pain will go away. You don't have to suffer with a loser like me.'

Sundhari calmly placed her hand on my chest and said, 'Don't give place to your negative feelings. Now, I can feel your heart. It beats the same but just fast. You won't lose yourself, Gautham. You won't let yourself do such a thing. I am with you on this journey. You have to be kind to yourself. Do what your therapist has told you to do at times like this. Remember the training.'

Her touch on my heart made me break out of the grief stuck inside me and I screamed. Gradually I tried to slow down my crying. The rain was so cold and I was trembling now. My teeth began to chatter.

'Breathe, Gautham! Breathe!'

I stood up slowly and asked her to go inside and dry herself up. She didn't bother what I said and continued to hold my hand.

With a mild tone, she said, "Come! Let's go inside."

Episode #3

THIRD time's a Charm

Do you know Sundhari?

Almost two years ago, Sundhari joined as a fresher at a mid-sized software development company. Her office had been the best escape from all the unrealistic pressures she had faced since childhood.

Despite being a girl keen on researching Medical Imaging, she was given the choice of doing only Engineering in Computer Science and was taken for granted and expected to continue to put her 100 per cent wherever she was. Dealing with the heartbreak of living in a place she never felt at home, she travelled quite a lot when she could. Sundhari often complained to her friend about exhausting her casual leaves of one year by the end of 6 months.

Sundhari's childhood was a battleground, a place where love had been replaced by the bitter stench of toxicity. Her parents' constant pushes painted the walls of their home with despair, leaving Sundhari yearning for an escape. With each passing day, she grew weaker and stronger at the same time, quietly vowing to break free from the chains that bound her. The parents who were supposed to lend their ears to their child were often seen-zoning her wishes, interests, hobbies and boundaries.

On her 24th birthday, Sundhari made a decision that would alter the course of her life. With a bag packed with dreams and a heart full of determination, she left her toxic home behind, the creaking door marking the beginning of her journey to freedom.

'Amma! Acha! There's a reason I chose this job. Yes, it is far from here. Maybe I'll find a home in the place I go. But I guess, I'd at least be able to do things for myself from tomorrow. You can now happily play with the joystick as always. But always remember that the PlayStation has already moved out of range.'

Alone but undeterred, Sundhari found herself a small 1 BHK apartment and a job that almost paid all her bills. The challenges she faced were numerous, but her spirit remained unbroken.

Sundhari happily embraced the solitude, using it as a canvas to paint the life she had always yearned for. Earning good friends at work as a fresher was almost as perfect too, because coincidentally her college friend worked there. Meanwhile, that friend's parents called her home every time she wanted to eat a nice Naadan meal. Her brother often took good care of her.

As the days turned into months, Sundhari carved a path of success for herself. Her hard work and resilience led her to opportunities she had never imagined. She enrolled in evening classes, pursuing a passion that had been stifled for far too long. Her tutor was a radiologist. Sundhari was no longer defined by the shadows of her past.

Amidst the chaos of self-discovery, Sundhari encountered Gautham on a random day at lunch. He was unlike anyone she had ever known – compassionate, understanding, and a beacon of support. They saw strength and support in each other and the relationship shaped up so perfectly like a puzzle.

As Sundhari continued to conquer the challenges that life threw at her, Gautham stood by her side, unwavering in his support. The toxic echoes of her past were replaced by the harmonious melody of their shared dreams and aspirations.

Sundhari's journey from a toxic home to a life of independence and love became an example she looked upon.

Her story was one of resilience, self-discovery, and the transformative power of genuine love. This may not be just how they found each other in the midst of chaos but just by being themselves and yet loving each other unconditionally.

Few months before

Sundhari and Gautham had been dating for a couple of months and it was Gautham's birthday.

Sundhari was talking to her friend in the evening. It was raining after a hot sunny day. The day had extracted so much energy out of her and as soon as the sky was covered with clouds and lit up with a flash of lightning, she called her friend via WhatsApp. The winds were not chill enough to cool down her home but yet she enjoyed the weather.

'*Edi*! I sent you the picture of all the gifts right? But I feel something is still missing!'

Her friend Rukmini replied, 'You've got so much Suna! Why do you feel that way?'

Sundhari hesitated, 'I just don't know *di*. Maybe!'

Rukmini interrupted, 'Look, Suna! You two are seeing each other. And it feels like you wanna do something memorable for him.'

Sundhari - 'Yeah! Memorable, yes! But what? I do not know.'

Rukmini spoke after a brief silence and a sneeze, 'Why don't you knock on his door with all the gifts you got for him? You know! Be his Santa Claus.'

Sundhari squealed in joy and agreed to it. She immediately decided that she was going to surprise him at 12 in the night. After placing all the gifts in a huge cardboard box and further wrapping the box in gift wrapping paper, she learnt from him that he was staying back in his apartment as his friends were out of town to go party.

She had a few more hours and right before dinner, she started writing him a letter.

Sundhari was positive that she was gonna skip eating food.

Dear Gautham,

Happy birthday, da! This is probably the first letter I am writing to you ever since we've known each other. Meeting you has been a good part of last year. But getting to know you has so far been the best part of this year. As you celebrate another year of life, my heart swells with gratitude for the gift of you. May your day be filled with all the love, joy, and happiness that you bring into my life every single day. May your dreams take flight on wings of possibility, and may your heart be filled with the knowledge that you are deeply cherished and adored.

Alright, enough with formalities! Thank you for making me believe in something other than solitude. I still love it but meeting you was like Wingardium Leviosa. Spirits lifted!

A butterfly choosing to sit on a peaceful human is quite natural. And feeling safe, confident with you, is natural too...The moment you held my hand, was quite magical... I never knew I'd find someone in a place I never really wanted to be in. Truly, we find the best humans in odd times. Exactly, when I wasn't looking. Like I said earlier once, maybe life is giving me a chance and showing me that I can forgive myself and let someone inside...Which made me think that it's worth it to walk with you. I love that you have the energy of a Hummingbird. Chirpy to talk to, has a personality as colorful as its neck and wants to hold my hand whenever it comes to me. I love birds, and so such a description.

If that movie Jawan had not been released, I'd not have come to the mall and you wouldn't have asked me out. So, I'm thanking Shah Rukh Khan for us. I am eternally grateful for the bond we share and the memories we're creating, and I cannot wait to continue this journey with you by my side.

I should stop before I blabber something so early! Anyway!

Here's to a bombastic, fantastic next year and I wish to support you, in ways I can... Here's to learning, and growing together and oh yeah! to roasting you :)

With Peace and Fun,

Sundhari :)

Episode #4

FOUR moments

After the hospital

'Yo! Where are we going? Just don't let me walk so much ok? I'm just so hungry and tired right now.'

I laughed like a Grinch for no reason and her eyebrows rose high hearing my weird laugh.

'We are going to this one cafe. And since it's past lunchtime, I'd prefer this one too. They have some friendly options for you.'

She stared at me just smiling. I wonder what was running through her mind. I felt breathless and maybe it was me who was running on her mind. The results were okay for now and for certain reports, we were asked to arrive the next day also to get checked with the doctor.

'Gautham?'

'Hm?'

'Would you still take me tomorrow to the hospital?'

'Sure. Why not?'

She chuckled and gently tapped on my shoulders and said to me joyfully, — 'Just kidding yaar! I'll go. I know you have to work, my workaholic friend. I'll take care of it tomorrow. I have a feeling that I'll get better today. And we are not there yet, so!'

'Yeah! We are not there yet. 2 more kilometres to go.'

'Such a nerd you are, asshole!'

A few minutes later at the cafe

I was fascinated by the vibe of this cafe even though I had come here with my friends many times. For some weird reason, they had made this cafe dark-themed so it still required candles and lights in mid of the day.

It was already 4 PM now.

As we sat at the table, I couldn't help but feel a sense of excitement inside me as I looked at her tired but beautiful face in that low yellow light that hung above us. I was just captivated by Sundhari's presence and was grateful to have met her. Even if this was my life's last minute, I might not have any regrets because I got to know someone like her.

Nah, that's a bit much.

'Worth it bro!'

I was totally amazed by this impeccable timing of hers but you have to know she meant it for the cafe's ambience and not for my inner monologue.

'Yeah. Like you... uh.. your name! Sundhary'

She had a silent but bellyful laugh, 'You fumbled a pickup line. hehehe!'

Well, we had a really wonderful conversation about a lot of random stuff in our lives. Most of the time, she spoke and I listened. I couldn't tell the time but I was sure many hours would have passed.

'Alright, let's go home, nah? You need to take some rest today.'

I paid the bill as I told her.

We walked outside and the steps led to the small garden path which further led to the entrance. It was all beautified and lit up so beautifully. It wasn't this gorgeous when we arrived.

'Gautham! Just wait,' she said and grabbed my hand to stop me from walking away.

'It has been a while since I had such a good time. And never have I felt so good. You made me feel good even at the time I was feeling sick. You're a good man, Gautham. You made my day.'

As usual, I was at a loss for words. But I didn't let myself stop.

'Sundhari! The feeling is mutual. I was just very concerned that you came out of your home even when you were not feeling well to meet me and I had to do something from my side. So, I thought — what's better than taking you to the hospital? Crazy idea but it was a good time. Drive slowly ok? Text me when you reach.'

'You know that it takes less than 10 minutes for me to reach my home.'

We giggled like kids and all of a sudden our eyes met. Wow, her eyes were like a crystal. Almost as if a white marble was painted with dark sky blue and fresh green algae. She didn't even need fancy contact lenses to flex her eye colour. Time seemed to slow down like in the movies. I could feel my heartbeat rising every second she inched closer to me. My lungs refused to work naturally. She grabbed my right hand and kept it behind her back, and then she held onto my shoulders. As I closed my eyes, our lips met and time completely stopped.

It was a tender, magical moment that conveyed all the unspoken emotions we had felt throughout the day. With that simple gesture, I knew this was the beginning of something special.

As we pulled away, I looked into her eyes and said, "That was..." My lungs which were in manual mode never let me say another word and she completed my sentence, "Beautiful!" and she held my cheeks for 2 seconds and walked away.

I stood there motionless with my mouth slightly open in awe, my heart almost trying to break out of my ribcage. A mildly chill breeze hit me while also swiping off the dry leaves and sand on the footpath.

Some months later, again!

As usual, I had already packed all my things, and since it was going to be at least 6 months — I had my trolley and the trekking bag ready. The night before, I was making our dinner while she packed her stuff.

'Baaaabe!' she yelled out and I knew exactly what she was searching for.

I screamed from the kitchen — 'It's in your dress cupboard's attic. Use the ladder.'

Minutes later I could hear her footsteps thudding towards the kitchen. She kept one hand on the wall and stared at me.

'Yeah, I just saw what you were packing, Sundhari. And I kept it in the attic 2 months ago and you still did not need it. Till now! And even now that's not inside your bag. It's almost near your bag and you came here to ask me if you really want to take it.'

'Yes, Mr. Know-It-All! Now tell me, shall I still...' She cutely groaned at me and continued, 'You know what! That's up to me to decide.'

I let out a sniffly laugh as she walked away.

After some time we had our dinner and then we finished up all the packing. We checked the house for things I might have left open. I was so tired of all the work and asked her, 'Baby! Can I go to sleep?'

'Please do, my love! You've done a lot. I'll just finish up this last episode in 2 minutes and come.'

5 minutes later, she came in, sat next to me on our bed and spoke softly,

'Gautham! I love you da.'

I was lying on the bed next to her and kept one hand on her cheek — 'Love you too, Sundhari! You also sleep. There's a long journey ahead.'

She switched off the lights and we cuddled inside one blanket in that cold room.

Morning Alarm rang

Sundhari switched off her alarm and woke up. She turned to see that Gautham was already up. 'Of course, he is a morning person!' she said and walked into the bathroom.

Sundhari came out and went to the hall. It was empty and she checked the kitchen as well. It was also squeaky clean.

'Baby?' she called out to Gautham.

She ran and checked in the bedroom too — 'Gautham! Are you in here?' and she knocked on the bathroom door.

'Gautham! Ennavane, Evde poye da. This is the second time you're freaking me out so much. GAUTHAM!'

(Gautham, my man. Where have you gone?)

Walking back to the hall and peeking at the balcony, she saw his mobile phone near the TV. She sighed a breath of relief as soon she saw his AirPods lying near his phone.

Suddenly, under the phone, she spotted his letter written with his Parker pen which was also sitting near the letter. A chill ran down her spine and her heart paced faster while she took the letter. Her hands shivered in fear. It read,

Anbe Sundhari,

The first thing I wanna say is, I am sorry! It has been so hard and I appreciate your love and care for me even after going through such things. Your entry into my life was like that first ray

of sunlight in the morning. So fresh and full of joy. I know just like that moment you should also be cherished.

I stand now in the eye of the storm and do not feel so good that you also are compelled to go through this. You have always told me that we are in this together. But deep inside I realise that this is my suffering and not yours. I am just trying to get better and until I think I have a grip on it; I am unable to see myself not taking care of you. This is a highway and I am standing on the express lane. It pains me to see you take so much effort. Your career is just starting and this trip will sabotage it if you are coming with me. I want you to promise me while you read this that no matter what, you will excel and I promise you while I write this — I love you no matter what. I would like to meet you again, as a better man than I ever was.

I hope you understand that I am not trying to push you away but I will contact you once I start my treatment. We will talk every single day, my love. I left my phone here for you and took my old flip phone and sim card. I dunno where this travel is going to take me now. By the time you read this, I will be far from our home. But I will never be far from my home — You!

The will to strive to find my own voice like you always said. But you waited long enough, Sundhari. Go get it, girl! Sundhari, you have been my guiding light, my rock, and my source of inspiration. Your presence in my life has brought me immeasurable joy, and I am eternally grateful for that.

Although I will miss you dearly, I also believe that this time apart will allow us to grow individually. Remember, my love, that you are always in my thoughts. I carry your love with me wherever I go, and it gives me the strength to face each day with optimism and determination. Please take care of yourself while I am away, and know that I eagerly await the day when we can be reunited once again. Until then, let our love be a guiding force in our lives, reminding us of the beauty and strength that exist within us.

Until then, with all the love,
Gautham :)

Episode #5
FIFTH gear

Sundhari was still in shock. She was left speechless and as she read the letter again, tears rolled down her face. She dropped down hard on the bean bag near her and kept the paper in the same place she took it. She slid down on the bean bag and stared at the ceiling with tears not stopping from her eyes.

Gautham could have said prior or convinced her that he needed to take this alone. The sudden move of his shook her. She was furious at him and equally missed him.

Her mind also wandered around her memories, and with all the gestures he had done, this was a dick move. But maybe he needed an escape. Not from Sundhari, not from love, and not from life. He needed to escape from the person he was living his life as.

All the memories of packing things, his funny anecdotes, the laughs they shared, the small playful fights, and everything from the last week preparing for this trip came in front of her eyes. Slowly, she tried to talk to herself but something obstructed her throat. The guilt, grief, and powerlessness of that moment burst out in the form of an outpour. Sundhari began to cry loudly.

She screamed, 'GAUTHAM!'

Some months ago after the first date at the hospital, again

Sundhari had called me in the afternoon while I was at the office during lunch break.

'Hey, man!'

She chuckled, 'What? Are your friends nearby? Don't worry. I'm not gonna flirt.'

'Haha! Thank god. Yeah, not now please.'

'Before you say something, I know you offered to go to the hospital now but actually, I had already visited in the morning. And also got the hard copies of the reports now. The doctor asked me to exercise regularly and there is nothing wrong with the scan reports. They had some doubt that there was a lump in the intramammary lymph nodes. So! The good news is, it's not there and I am healthy.'

'Oh! Somehow I knew you were alright. Anyway! How's your fever now?'

She grinned and said, 'It was fine since morning. But talking to you, I am feeling it again bro! Maybe because of your hotness.'

'Alright, there it comes! I'll call you in a while dude. Finishing up my lunch now.'

'Oo! Okay man, see ya.'

Some months later, again!

As I drove to Bangalore or nowhere, I was still guilty of leaving my love behind. It drove me crazy but I didn't want to be her burden. Being in love was to be with each other in all circumstances. The circumstances seemed to be too far now and I could not be like that and watch how much she was trying. It killed me every day but then my anxiety killed me from the inside.

I had bought my uncle's old Mahindra Scorpio which was still in mint condition after years of maintaining it so preciously.

It tore me apart to even think about leaving her behind — the woman who had been my constant support and confidante for a year now.

'Yet I hope that by embarking on this journey, I'd be able to find a way to reconcile my guilt and emerge stronger. Be with her, by being 100% myself!'

I had taken only my backpack and left all my formal clothes behind in my suitcase along with my heart — who I thought would be so angry with me right now. I consoled myself as I slowly drove into the parking of the cafe on the side of the highway. It was a Cafe Coffee Day.

I walked in to order a simple cappuccino and sat at the place closest to the road so that I could stare outside and also write my journal. As I stared at the incoming and outgoing traffic through the tinted glass, I felt someone approach me.

The barista was coming towards me with a cappuccino and a sandwich.

'Thank you, sir! But I didn't order a sandwich.'

The barista smiled — 'You are our first order today morning sir. So, we always offer a sandwich to our first customer. I forgot to mention this while taking your order. Hope this is fine for you.'

'Yeah, that's fine. I'll take it. Thank you very much, sir!'

It was warm, and cheesy and had spinach and corn reminding me of the sandwich she made me one time.

Back at home

Sundhari picked up his phone and looked at the lock screen of both of them smiling and holding hands in front of a lake during sunset. It was the most peaceful picture to look at. She then unlocked his phone and went through the contacts.

She said to herself — 'If only you could answer me right away. You left your phone here! Why would you go alone, my baby? I could have come with you. Are you doing okay?'

She called his sister from her phone and spoke casually just to know if he was there and found out he was not. She spoke to his sister for a while about random stuff.

'Okay, bye ma. Talk to you soon.'

Suddenly, she was reminded of someone and scrolled his contacts again; she found his friend's number and rang him up. Unfortunately, since that guy was on the night shift, he might have just come home and slept. So, she immediately cut the call. Then, she said, 'Should I call his therapist? Maybe he would have mentioned something!'

Sundhari was worried about him.

At the Highway Cafe

While I was halfway through my large cup of cappuccino, I realized it wasn't worth it and should have ordered a hot chocolate instead. The thing about me going through anxiety was, I was not supposed to have coffee. My palpitations would be triggered. Well, it had been so many months since I had a coffee and I would be fine. I might use this adrenaline shoot-up for my drive.

The cafe was right next to a petrol station and I saw a woman driving in an old but funky-looking Maruthi 800 and arriving at the pump. The car wasn't starting after filling up. Three people who worked at the petrol station helped her push the car towards the parking space, towards the side under the shade and she thanked them and started to look under the hood. After a couple of minutes of inspection, she shut the hood and took out her backpack from the backseat, locked her car, and started walking towards the cafe.

She walked into the cafe and instantly asked for a cold coffee and looked for a table. She acknowledged me with a smile and there was a sofa, one table away in front of me — and sat there. She had a medium-sized, around 60-liter backpack with many badges and pins, and keychains hanging around and wore a simple outfit of grey denim pants, a pastel blue pullover shirt, and an ink-blue denim jacket.

'Solo-ing out here in this wonderful moody weather?' she asked.

I didn't expect her to talk but this took me by surprise and I couldn't state the reason.

'Yeah! Well, I planned something. Doing something else.'

'That's relatable! Where are you up to?'

She looked like a very confident and smart lady. She must be older than me.

'Honestly! Now I have no idea. Per plan, it was Bengaluru but now I don't know where I am going. Couldn't figure it out yet. Where are you going?'

'To see my mom for the last time. She lives in north Telangana, the place where my dad was working.'

'Oh! But your car... I .. uh.. Can I look into it for you?'

She smirked and chuckled. 'Thanks! But I.... I know my way around things. And that cool-looking car has to stay there until a heart transplant is done. I mean, the engine seized up and I guess the third time is not the charm for this baby. Requires a lot of work to get her back up. But it can be fixed, unlike relationships.'

'I'm sorry, I don't follow you.'

'That's fine! You don't have to be sorry. I recently signed the papers for separation. The guy wasn't as supportive as I thought. And......... Ah! Here comes the saviour. Thank you for the cold-coffeeeeee!"

She had one sip and she enjoyed it like it was her first ever cold coffee. "Wow! The coffee is fantastic."

The barista replied from behind the counter, 'Thank you so much, ma'am!'

This reminded me of Sundhari who always tried to go to the counter of any restaurant and give credit to the one who made her food. As I smiled at nothing, the lady asked me, 'Hmm! A good memory jog? Let me guess, your wife?'

'Um! No, we aren't married yet. She is uhn... She's the best! But uh, I left her back so that her life does not become drab like mine.'

She thought for a moment and said — 'Hmm! Do say a "hi" on my behalf the next time you speak to her!'

After a short silence, I said to her — 'My name is Gautham!'

She took her coffee, came to my table, sat opposite me and gave me her hand. We shook hands while she said, "I'm Venba! Hi! Do you mind dropping me somewhere? If it's okay for you.'

'Uhn, Yeah! Yeah! Sure I can drop you...urm... where?'

She looked outside to the road while it was drizzling, took a sip of her cold coffee, and said, 'Hmm! Near! I'll tell you when. It's on the way.'

She smiled brightly while I tried too. One could recognize my fake smile, a mile away.

Episode #6

It's a SIX!

A lightbulb moment had hit her. It was staring right at her face but she was blinded by thoughts about him. With shaking hands and fumbling breath, she dropped the phone from her hands onto the floor, picked up the letter, and read it again.

...We will talk every single day, my love. I left my phone here for you and took my old flip phone and sim card...

'Gautham.. Gautham!'

With so much rush and her fingers trembling in mixed emotions, she tapped on so many wrong options, and finally, she rang his number.

Two rings and it said that the user was busy. She tried again and heard the same thing after a few rings.

'Gautham! PICK UP!' She fell on her knees on the floor and started to weep and threw the letter across the hall. Due to the fan in the hall running at full speed, it flew across and floated in the air. Dropping her phone, she kept both her hands on her face and started to weep loudly in the child's pose. The floating letter hit her head and landed in front of her face.

Wiping tears off her face, she looked at the letter and the lines that caught her attention now,

...Although I miss you dearly, I also believe that this time apart will allow us to grow individually. Remember, my love, that you are always in my thoughts. I carry your love with me wherever I go,...

With a feeble crying voice, she said to the letter in a louder voice, anger boiling over,

'I HATE YOU!'

She curled up on the floor hugging the letter — 'Oh, my budhdhu baby! Are you okay?' she quivered and continued, 'Gautham! I love you!'

At the parking outside the Cafe

Venba was surprised that the Scorpio was mine. While she was getting into the car she said, 'Bro! Such a great performance car. I was thinking who had this beauty maintained like this from 2009? It is you! Kudos to you man!'

With a mild unexciting voice, I said, 'Thank you!'

As I backed up the car from the parking and put on the seatbelts, my phone rang.

Ende Sundhari... My Sundhari

Calling...

I cut the call and continued to drive to the service road. Moments later, she called me again on my phone.

'Aren't you gonna pick it up, Gautham?'

I rejected the call again and put it on silent mode. 'I'm not ready now, I guess!'

Snickering, Venba said, 'No one ever is! Alright, Chalo! Let's go.'

Why did she reply that way, I would never know. She was a very deep person was what I could observe. After we drove silently for some time, she put on some songs using the AUX cord from her phone. She understood that I did not want to speak. I could feel that she was going through something but I let her tell me on her own and wait until that. I glanced at her and looked back at the road.

I could sense she was smiling when she asked — "What are you curious about?"

'A lot of things to be honest...'

And she immediately interrupted me, 'The random girl who asked you for a lift and you don't even know who she really is — was actually a girl with wonderful dreams and goals and partner and family and cats and whatnot. It was beautiful!'

She looked at me and softly continued, 'I guess!' and chuckled.

Some months ago when they met outside

Sundhari exclaimed — 'I didn't know. I had no idea how greedy my heart really was. Gautham! It haunts me, you know.'

She was so perplexed about what had happened last night. We had an argument about something very silly and it had been disturbing both of us. So we decided to meet each other and talk. We knew that we would find ourselves laughing about it; which, of course, was what we were doing before she said that. We still couldn't call ourselves boyfriend or girlfriend. We both had not confessed our love to each other.

A tear pooled in the corner of her eyes.

'Gautham?' and the tears rolled down her cheeks.

I wiped her tears, kept my hand on her cheeks and said, 'Remember the game we played last time you came to my home? That old game. It had some pink circles near the buildings. When we walk into those glowing circles, we stop playing and see a cutscene right? Our lives are filled with such pink circles. They just don't make themselves seen. Because we see them already. When we see them, we stop and see the cutscene of the past even if we don't want to.'

She nodded slowly and continued staring into my soul.

Sundhari - 'Say more!'

'What we can do is let those cutscenes end, with a little courage for one more time and play the game. If you don't want to, just take the car and drive *chumma.* When you feel like you are up for a mission, you can continue with new pink circles.'

She smiled with her eyes and I felt her cheeks widen through my palm. Sundari held my hand to her face, pulled it towards me, and kissed my palm. Then she chuckled, 'I gave you my first kiss!'

My heart skipped a beat. It began beating faster and I started staring at her. I took her hand and kept it on my chest. She laughed at how fast it was beating.

'What did you say?'

'I feel your heart! Um! Gautham! uhn....Wa..wa...HAAAA....What are we doing right now?' She took her hand away and looked at me and I could sense her breathing was heavy too. We tried to change the subject and speak something else. Our conversation began with ease, flowing effortlessly from one topic to another.

We laughed, shared stories, and discovered common interests. I found myself fascinated by the depth of Sundhari's thoughts and the sincerity with which she spoke. But there was a moment when Sundhari's tone changed, and I sensed that something significant was about to be revealed.

She spoke about the hardships in her life which she hasn't yet revealed to me. I was just sitting there, listening to her speak.

My heart ached as I listened to Sundhari's story unfold; sensing the weight she had carried and the scars she bore from her past. But amidst the darkness of her past, I saw a glimmer of resilience and determination. I saw a person who had overcome immense obstacles and still managed to radiate kindness and compassion.

As Sundhari finished recounting her past, there was a brief silence between us. We did not look at each other. I somehow knew that my response at that moment would shape our relationship. I reached out, gently took Sundhari's hand in mine, and looked into her eyes.

At first, my voice broke, but I cleared my throat and started to speak.

'Sundhari! Thank you for sharing such a deeply personal part of your life with me. I want you to know that I'm honoured that you trust me enough to confide in me. Your past doesn't define you; it's proof of your strength and resilience. I just want you to know that I am here for you for exactly who you are.'

Sundhari's eyes welled up with tears, and I could see a mixture of relief and gratitude in her expression. At that moment, we both knew that our connection had deepened, and the bond had become even stronger.

She hugged me very tightly for the first time. She let go of me, wiped her tears, and spoke with a shaky, soft voice.

'Gautham! It feels that my heart knows that it found someone truly special. The one with whom I dare to open up and be vulnerable, and someone who looks through me, with my past. Now, here... Sitting with you, I feel complete. A profound satisfaction and gratitude. Would you want this to continue, forever?'

Hearing this, everything went silent. Or too loud! I felt my watch ticking. I felt my breath leaving the lungs through my nose. A tiny sound exited my mouth before I responded,

'Sundhari! I love you!'

Episode #7
SEVEN wonders

During the drive to somewhere after Coffee

It had been 2 hours since we started from the cafe and we barely spoke about anything. Venba started to talk about something but she got a call and then we stayed silent afterwards.

I asked while looking at the road, 'Are you okay?'

She looked at me to answer with a smile, 'To burn with desire and keep quiet about it is the greatest punishment we can bring ourselves.'

'So, don't punish yourself. Say it, no?'

'Gautham! I have been fending off the negativity all by myself since childhood. I had a very beautiful family but the pandemic stopped making it so beautiful. The last leg of my research days to get my second doctorate became a living hell due to that. Could have shown my dad that I did research on something I love. My dad loved Dostoevsky! I loved Shirley Jackson. He did multiple PhDs in Tamil and English Literature and I found love in Lit also since our home had a mini library and most of my childhood was spent playing in that room with toys and books.'

The needle on the speedometer began to droop. I reduced the volume of the music and it resembled a piece of background music from afar. Her voice was still strong even when she spoke about the tragedy. It was like she still had a lot of stories in her life to tell.

'I'm listening!' I said, clearing my throat.

'You know what? That statement which you said now — I'm listening. I wish my partner.. or rather ex-partner could have just done it for once. Everything could have become easier. He was the best. Maybe he still is, according to him.

But to me, love stopped trying. We both love to learn a new language, for fun. Sometimes I keep my feelings to myself because after our relationship was so mute, I couldn't find a language to describe it. Have you ever had days like that, Gautham?'

I switched lanes and went to the extreme left end of the road and began to tell her the answer — 'Ms. Venba. I uh..' and she interrupted me.

'Let's not have this Mr. Ms. business. Call me Venba!'

'Yes! Venba! We have had such days. When we both desperately wanted to share but did not have the energy to try. We take off somewhere individually — sometimes to our parents' home or somewhere like that. A couple of days later, we tend to stick to each other on return.'

'Have you ever stopped trying?'

'I once tried to stop myself, forever, but she pulled me out. Even now, I am in such a place that I have to get better first for myself, then for her. Maybe that's why I am here, driving to nowhere.'

She had a bellyful laugh and switched off the music — 'Gautham! I feel that you two are perfect for each other. It's only for the good that you are here alone. Trying to figure out something you don't know about. And don't worry, you're gonna be fine. She's, also gonna be fine. A little angry perhaps...'

I moved the car into the truck layover and opened the windows as the drizzling stopped. I gave her the reason for this drive.

'I am supposed to drive to Bengaluru. But this is taking me somewhere. Dealing with severe anxiety attacks and depressive episodes in my life, I got tired of inflicting pain on myself. I am unable to sit and watch my Sundhari also sacrificing some of her happy stuff because she had to be there for me. I know love is to be there for each other but too much sacrifice also hurts me a lot. She was supposed to come with me but since this is the beginning of her career, I didn't want to sabotage anything. She has to grow. I will be getting regular treatments in Bengaluru for which I even tried to quit my high-paying job but they let me go on sabbatical. I am so tired! What if Sundhari can never forgive me for leaving her behind.'

She tapped my shoulder twice and said, 'Look G! I cannot offer you any advice but always remember. She will forgive you for this. Of all the people, she still stood by you. It will take time for her to digest the fact that you came here alone, but she'll stand by you, always! She loved spending time with you even when you were not okay. You are a good person, man! Don't hear the voice in your head at such times. Humans have always found a way to figure it out. We always do!'

As soon as she said this, two people in a rather old diesel Bullet motorcycle arrived at the same truck layover spot. The guy who sat at the back seemed to be searching for something and then he noticed us in the car. Removing his helmet, he walked towards us and asked me to open the window. The other guy near the motorcycle seemed familiar!

Two months ago during dinner time at their home

Sundhari had been making his favourite corn, cheese and spinach sandwich which used to be much better than the ones he used to have in Cafe Coffee Day during the initial phase of their dating.

She said to herself softly— 'Gautham! You have cooked so many meals for me, but today, you gonna love this. Just like you asked, the CCD Sandwich. TADAA! GAUTHAM! Come here for a second, no?'

She paced to their bedroom and the bathroom door was ajar. She opened it to check whether he was in the bathtub and found that he was fully immersed in water except for the face. His right hand outside the tub was dripping water and blood. There was a puddle of blood and water on the floor where his hand hung out.

"Budhdhu! *Nee endhaada kaariyam cheyth...*"

(Budhdhu! What have you done?)

She rushed to pull him upwards and went on to observe his hand. He had cut his right-hand palm with a knife which he still held in his left hand under the water. She took the knife by force, threw it onto the floor, then pulled a dry towel that was hanging by the wall and tried to stop the bleeding. She was also now covered in his blood.

His eyes were red, his face was pale and dull without expression. He was still looking at the wall speechless. She sat on the edge of the bathtub, held him by his shirt, made him sit straight inside the tub, and took out the drain shoe. She got flustered and gave him a tight slap on the face.

He slowly looked at her and began to cry loudly on her lap.

'Get up, Gautham! Please come out. You are bleeding so much. I'm here! Come. Get up.'

Gautham stopped crying and with a broken voice, he uttered, 'You go Sundhari! I'm a dead weight.'

Her anger multiplied along with the volume of her voice, 'DEI! VAADA!'

After changing the clothes and getting his cut cleaned and dressed, he walked to the hall behind her. She made him sit on the dining table and he drank some water. Standing by his side, she kept her hand on his shoulders.

'Gautham! I want you to eat something. We are going to the hospital afterwards. Somehow the cut wasn't deep and now it has stopped bleeding. The dressed-up cotton bandages were reddish with blood. Consider yourself lucky that the doctor's family at the end of our hall was good enough to help you stitch it up.'

She brought the sandwiches and some leftover baked veggies from lunch, sat down next to him and said, 'Eat budhdhu!'

Tears welled up in Gautham's eyes as he looked at Sundhari, his voice filled with remorse. 'I uh... can't believe what almost happened, Sundhari,' he whispered, his voice barely audible. 'I'm sorry for putting you through this. I hurt you! I am hurting you so much, no?'

Sundhari gently placed her hand over his shoulders even though her hands were slightly shaking and he immediately put his arms around her. She held him with both her hands like a mother holding her child. His eyes were red from crying, while her gaze was filled with unyielding love. 'Gautham, don't apologize,' she choked out, with a voice filled with pain and continued with determination. 'I can't bear the thought of losing you. You are not alone in this, remember? You were there for me when I lost something valuable in my life. And you were there when I got my dream job. We face everything together.'

'I love you, Sundhari', Gautham whispered, his voice breaking. 'Your love saved me tonight. You saved me from the dirt of my own mind'.

Back to the car near the truck parking

The guy who came to talk to us was smiling and the way he started to talk to me made me believe he knew me for years. Venba immediately said, 'We'll just get outside. Let's talk in that tree shade!'

And he ran towards the bike and got the bag from him. While we were getting down and walking to the pavement, the person who rode the bullet took off leaving his pillion behind.

I panicked and said to the guy who was walking towards us, 'He's leaving?'

Venba chuckled, 'Yeah, I guess you have another passenger now.' For a traveller like him, the bag was very small and he started to enquire about how my route was and which way I would be taking.

'I uh actually...!' I peeked towards Venba with a questionable look, then continued. She nodded.

'I haven't decided. She actually is going to Telangana. So maybe I'll just drop her on my way. Where are you going?'

He laughed with such a bright face and body language. Scratching his beard, he said, 'Well, I'll get down on the way. The place is just near!'

Venba's voice was filled with gratitude — 'Gautham! Let him come, no? His friend also left. We'll have one more person to talk to.'

With a thoughtful nod, I said, 'Ok!'

A peal of bright laughter from him again. 'Let's know about each other. You seem to be a little tired and why don't I drive this beast? You know it's rare to see this edition of Scorpio on the roads nowadays.'

Venba took the keys from my hand and handed it over to him. He put his hand over my shoulders and walked along with me. A random stranger I met on the side of the highway wanted me to drop him wherever I decided and was filled with so much joy and positivity. This gentleman was a traveller going places where people needed him. Did the people call him out in the first place? Maybe not. It sounded like I was describing a superhero.

I was going to sit behind him in the second row while Venba sat as the front passenger. He and I opened the doors in sync and he said, 'Now sir! We are part of a flock. The flock of birds that wander.'

'I am a... bird?'

He gently hit me in the back and chuckled, 'Of course Mr. Vijay!'

'Umm! My name is Gautham!'

'Oh! Okay, Vijay!' for which Venba started to laugh. He inclined to rename people how he wanted. He lent his arm to me to shake hands. As we shook hands he said,

'Charlie!'

Episode #8
EIGHT pages

A*fter meeting Charlie during the drive* I sat in the back seat as Charlie confidently took the wheel. Venba, always the peacemaker, settled into the passenger seat. The car engine roared to life, and we set off on a road trip to a nearby hill station. He changed the routes, of course.

The initial silence was broken by Charlie's cheerful voice. 'So, guys, I'll tell you an embarrassing thing that happened to me.' 'I was with a thief,' he continued, a smile playing on his lips. 'We were gonna drop into the house through the tiled roof and saw that no one was in the house, the *kallan,* the thief, dropped me inside and he ran away because I accidentally told the police that he was a thief when we were walking on a New Year's Eve night. I was drunk so I don't even remember half of it.'

I chuckled and felt my mood lightening slightly. 'I'd fall inside even if the thief hadn't helped me!'

'Yeah!' Charlie continued. 'So there I was, trying to figure out what to do. I ended up having to climb through the bathroom window, which was slightly open. It was not my finest moment, but it makes for a good story!'

Venba chimed in, sharing her own funny mishap. As they shared stories of their embarrassing moments, I found myself laughing genuinely, while the dark mood slowly dissipated.

The car climbed higher, and we reached a beautiful viewpoint in a matter of hours. We parked the car and got out to take in the breathtaking scenery. The view of the valley below and the majestic mountains in the distance was awe-inspiring.

'Wow, this is amazing,' I said, finally finding the beauty in the world.

Charlie put an arm around my shoulders. 'See, buddy? *EE malagale pole, jeevitham pogunne vare, namakku ups and downs undaavum (Just like these mountains, until life ends life has its ups and downs). The worries and pain of the past will end soon.* At the end of this journey, I'll drop you folks at a place to stay for some time. I have to go somewhere after then.'

Venba nodded in agreement. 'And guess what! You have friends to support you through it all.'

As we continued the journey, Charlie and Venba continued to weave stories and jokes, so much so that I forgot my demons existed. I felt peaceful. Charlie stopped at a roadside *dhaba* for lunch, where they relished delicious local cuisine and bonded with the friendly staff.

Charlie was so friendly with everyone, even the people who ran the *dhaba*. One of the cooks even came to him and spoke for a long time about his family.

As we were sitting outside on a cot to eat, there was a person selling tea, coffee and snacks. Venba went to buy tea for herself and asked if I needed one.

I yelled from my place - 'Oru kattan madhi!'

(One black tea is enough for me)

Charlie from behind me, '*Ah, Venba, one black tea for me too. No sugar!*'

Charlie asked, 'So, what is the story behind that black tea, that *kattan chaaya*?'

I told him a memory from my heart that happened with Sundhari during our early dating days.

<u>*Many months before*</u>

Gautham texted Sundhari - 'Hey??'

Sundhari replied, 'Sorry da. Dumb days at work. I will call you by evening!'

Gautham - 'Okk! Anytime Wonderwoman!'

Sundhari - "Thanks da! Guess I needed that. Made me smile :) "

Juggling so much stuff inside his head and literally on hand, Sundhari's words got him through the rough start of his work day. Cooking lunch and simultaneously roasting colleagues at work for assigning him their tasks was how he was till lunchtime.

Being at home, he had got it cleaned and realized that while cleaning his home, he was becoming something else with all the rage and monstrosity he showed towards dirt and dust. Wow! That would be a fun anecdote for her. Seeing him lose his mind over a dust-pan would make her laugh. In the late afternoon, Sundhari called him, her voice carrying a hint of exhaustion. She suggested meeting for evening tea, a simple yet meaningful gesture that Gautham welcomed.

Eager to reconnect with Sundhari and provide the support she needed, he agreed to the plan.

Later they met at one of the tea shops near her office campus. Although it was tea time, it was not very crowded. Ordering black tea for himself, he ordered a low-sugar strong masala tea for Sundhari.

Sundhari - "Podhum podhum!" (Enough, Enough)

Gautham with an Italian hand gesture, 'A warm gesture perhaps?'

Sundhari tapped his shoulders, 'You are here. That's warm enough. 'Let's sit there,' she said and pointed to a bench nearby. She sat first. The tea was already prepared. Picking it up from the counter, Gautham brought it to the table and sat in front of her. They hit cheers and started to sip.

Gautham slyly said, 'Had it been a colder one!' for which she just shook her head. And zoned out while sipping her soul-touching tea.

Halfway through, he double-tapped her wrist and asked in a hand gesture - 'Are you okay?'

She moved a bit and tapped on the bench, 'You come and sit here'

He almost tripped but managed not to fall, went, and sat next to her. She scooched towards him and laid her head on his shoulders - 'Gautham?'

'Yes?'

'I'm feeling so restless. I could not go to my friends because I wanted this calmness. They do everything they can to cheer me up. But I am not feeling glee. So glum!'

And she put her hand onto his and entangled their arms. With a slight hesitation, he patted her hand.

'Your hands are so warm da!'

Tapping the tea glass, he indicated that it might be due to the hot tea. She peeked at his face, dropped her head again onto his shoulders and said, 'Don't over-explain, man! Ok, listen!'

'Hmm?!'

And Sundhari started ranting about her office, her manager who did not stand up for her, and the random tasks that she got burdened with, which were not even hers to begin with. But he made sure he had given ears to Sundhari's non-stop bludgeoning of her rough days at work.

A small silence later, he asked if she wanted to say something else. She was so tired, that she almost would have dozed off. The sense of calm she felt around him was unbelievable even for her.

As time passed by, the atmosphere began to shift. Gautham could sense Sundhari gradually letting go of the burdens that had weighed her down. It wasn't just about the tea or the casual setting; it was about the connection they shared and the solace found in each other's company. By this time, including the one other customer, only three people were in the tea shop.

Sundhari - 'Dei!'

Sundhari looked at Gautham with gratitude in her eyes. 'You make me feel safe,' she confessed. Those simple words carried profound meaning, encapsulating the security and comfort she found in their relationship. Gautham was touched by her sincerity, a silent affirmation of his commitment to being her anchor in times of turbulence. With zero hesitation, he patted her hand.

Gautham spoke now, 'You deserve all the praise, Sundhari. With all such hard work you've been doing and still do. I'm proud of you!'

She lifted her head from his shoulders, still holding his arms, she said, 'Good boy! 100 marks. Come! Take me around in your bike.'

He decided and asked if they could go to the mall just for a ride. It was almost just 10 kilometres on the straight highway. She giggled and messed up his neatly set-back hair.

This time, she held his shoulders and playfully massaged him saying his shoulders were tight. While they stopped at a signal, she came near his ears and said, 'Don't dream, just drive' and laughed.

He replied, 'Never resisting one opportunity to roast me, eh?'

'Yoo dude! Definitely. That's my love language.'

After some open roads, warm winds, and a couple of traffic signals, they returned to the tea shop where she had parked her vehicle. She gave him such a stylish fist-bump to a handshake. No grand gestures or elaborate promises were needed; the silent understanding between them spoke volumes. Near that quiet tea shop, surrounded by a ginormous almond tree, they rediscovered the strength that came from facing challenges together.

As they left the cafe, the night air felt lighter, and the burden of thc day lifted. Gautham and Sundhari walked hand in hand, the unspoken assurance of their bond shining brighter than ever. In the simple act of sharing tea and conversation, they found a refuge in each other, a sanctuary where vulnerability only strengthened the foundation of their yet-to-be-discovered bond.

He wore his helmet and walked towards his bike. She said in a louder voice, 'Gautham!'

Tossing the helmet on the side mirror, he walked towards her again, 'What?'

'Nothing! Drive safe and hey! Thanks, da. Honestly, I feel lighter and I can quote again what I said that day. You are a nice company to be with.'

At that moment, amidst the aroma of tea and the soft glow of the cafe's lights, he kept his right hand over his heart and said, 'Anytime, Sundhari! Reach me when you text'

She laughed brightly and said, "Ok. Clumsy fellow!" and only then he realised what he had said.

Back in the hills with Charlie and Venba

Throughout the day, Charlie drove through unknown cities and routes showing us so many picturesque spots and interesting people, as we laughed over silly jokes, and even sang together during the drive. The camaraderie between us was palpable, and it was evident that we cherished each other's company. So hard to think how it would have been solo, now.

As evening descended, we found ourselves in the village. I now felt grateful for the memorable day shared with Charlie and Venba.

'You know what, guys?' I said with a newfound lightness in my voice. 'Thank you for today. I really needed this.'

Charlie gave out a hearty and bright laugh. 'Anytime, my friend.'

Venba nodded. 'Remember, life is full of random moments, both good and bad. It's important to cherish the good ones and lean on your friends during tough times. The ones worthy enough will stay by your side even from afar. Second chances don't appear so often! Trust me, I know.'

Stopping at an old-age home at the top of the estate, Charlie gave us both a tight, warm hug. A woman, probably of my age, walked towards us, while he walked away towards the road waving his hand in the air.

Venba asked her — 'By the looks of everyone. I see this ain't the first time.'

The woman replied, 'He's rescued so many souls. The most damned ones. He's touched the minds of people that it left them speechless for good. I see that your friend is also experiencing such euphoria. Don't worry! He'll be back' and everyone started to walk inside while the house-help Marudhu asked us to accompany him to his room.

I asked the woman, 'When will he return?' for which she only smiled. Is he a guardian angel in disguise?

As I walked into this home, I realized that while life could be unpredictable and challenging, having people like Charlie and Venba by my side made the journey worthwhile. Their support and laughter reminded me that joy and happiness could always be found, even in the moments we never wanted it.

A couple of weeks before

I had returned from my last day at the office before I went to Bengaluru for my treatments. My team had been so kind and cooperative in everything. Even though I said I may return to them in a year, some of my folks were really emotional too. There were almost 10 days till I left. I felt so heavy and weird about leaving a place Sundhari and I called home. It was one of our dreams to move into such a place. Selling my old land back in my hometown, more than half of the settlement was already done and I loaned the remaining money.

This house was suggested by my manager who was actually planning to buy it but passed it on to us. The balcony is still our favourite place to chill out.

Sundhari was sitting on the balcony in her favourite bean bag working on something on her laptop.

'Babe!'

'Budhdhuuuuuu! You are home! Freshen up yourself. We need to go out somewhere.'

To my surprise, she said we were going to dinner at my favourite cafe near the cliff. It had been at least a month since I went there as it was a little far from the place we lived. I used to love their cappuccino and cold coffee but once I quit coffee, I discovered that their tea was fantastic too.

Tea along with the sound of waves crashing during sunset was such a beautiful experience until Sundhari came along. Since that time, the experience elevated more.

At the cafe after an hour or so

As the sun began its descent, casting a warm golden hue across the beach, Sundhari and I sat at our favourite cafe near the cliff overlooking the magnificent view. The salty breeze gently brushed against her hair, carrying with it the sweet aroma of the sea.

For once, I was jealous that the wind had more liberty than me. Her dewy eyes when hit with the orange rays of the sun, were just something so... I'd say wow!

But witnessing all these, suddenly out of the blue, I asked her, 'Why do you have to do so much for me?'

Sundhari — 'I know you really didn't want to ask me that question but still. The thing is however we are, you mean so much to me in my life. I am so glad our paths crossed and this is just one small gesture that we both do to each other. Sometimes it feels like you don't even deserve it but that's just your inner voice not saying what it should. Even if we were just friends, I'd show the same care and affection towards you.'

I was feeling so emotional because of the last day at the office and somehow I asked her such a stupid question.

'Sometimes you show me so much love that it feels like I'm floating in the sky. But when I do not have control, it feels as if I don't deserve this much love. I'm talking crazy just...... let's not talk about it. Never realized how much of this is my fight and not yours. I am so sorry!'

She patted and rested her hand on my shoulder and said, 'Budhdhu! You'll figure this out da. Don't worry. Whatever that inner voice is telling you, don't listen to it. If I have to be honest, Yes! The fights and the efforts are yours. I'm just your cheerleader, supporter, fan, well-wisher, or whatever you call it. More than everything, a good friend who knows you so well and wants to be there for you. I love how much you put effort into getting better. It's a long way. But you can do this Gautham! And to celebrate and appreciate those efforts, I have brought you here.'

We were talking so much about our dreams, and the goals we want to accomplish, and my fears also came up when a big-ass spider crawled across behind the glass wall of the cafe.

'Stupid spider!'

She is indeed my greatest pillar of strength even when the times are testing us. I felt so grateful for her unwavering support. Lost in the beauty of the moment, Sundhari and I marvelled at the magnificence of nature. We held hands, feeling the warmth and reassurance in each other's touch. In that serene setting, we found comfort and peace, a brief respite from the chaos of the world.

As the sun dipped below the horizon, leaving behind a trail of glowing embers, we somehow knew we would always cherish the memory. It was a moment of love, connection, and appreciation, a reminder of the strength we found within ourselves and each other.

Clouds were dark yet the hint of pink and orange colours were seen across. Like a shooting star, a person from behind said — 'I just wanna say — I see so much admiration between the two of you enjoying each other's company. I see so much love between the two of you in such a magnificent backdrop — it feels like a symphony.'

That man had such a warm smile and we couldn't help but admire his words and acknowledge him with a smile. He wore such hippie clothes and a tie-dye hoodie which made us assume he was a guy living off travel and friendships.

He pulled up a chair to our table with a cup in his hand and introduced himself — 'Hi! My name is Mani Maaran. But you can call me Maara.'

Episode #9

NINE-NINE

D*inner time after Charlie left the village*

We witnessed one of the most beautiful sunsets from the mountain where a person from this old-age home took me and Venba in a Jeep. He spoke in Tamil. It was so amazing to see Venba speaking so fluently. Back in the old-age home, she spoke in Marathi to a young girl who said so many things about plants. She had mentioned that somehow since childhood she had a habit of picking up the language of the place she visited.

That man Marudhu told so many stories about Charlie and how he was literally an angel on earth and yet he always vanished just like today.

I helped in the kitchen while Venba had been busy talking to some of the people staying there. I helped them make a nice dal makhani for the chapatis. One of the people who worked in the kitchen asked me if I had someone in my life. She was so warm and appreciated how I was good at seasoning the dal.

'Suhana Ammae! I live with my girlfriend. We are not still married and I have come on this journey.'

Marudhu entered the kitchen and said in a fake angry voice to that lady — 'Suhana ma! Adhu ellam Gautham sir kitta kekadheenga. Avarum nammala maadri Charlie thaan vitutu ponaaru.' He looked at me and said, 'Sir! Thappa eduthukadheenga!'

(*Don't ask those questions to Gautham. Charlie has brought him here just like us................Sir! Please don't feel bad about it*)

The lady replied to me, 'You will get the answer you are searching for. Eventually, we always do. I am sorry, *mone*!'

I said raising my palm — 'Achacho Suhana ma! It's okay. It's cool. And thank you!'

Later during dinner time, we all went to the dining center which was first constructed as a prayer hall for the home. The place was so vibrant with the old people from the home, children who were rescued by Charlie, the gardening couple with their son, and the two of us. Many thought I was a chef and I was happy to have made something delicious for them.

One old man named Kunjappan who seemed to share the knowledge of God told us many stories about the home. I slowly started to feel my anxiety attack seeping in. Venba noticed I was so nervous that I began to shake my leg or tap the table with my finger strangely.

Kunjappan was telling us the story of how he met his first crush some months ago and how he felt like he was 20 again in his 70s.

Suhana, whom I worked with, in the kitchen came to my left and held my hand. 'Mone! Come with me.'

We walked towards the fireplace behind the house on the cold night where everyone used to gather for some time after dinner. She asked if I wanted to express something as she noticed my strange behaviour at the table.

'Suhana ma! I feel like I want an immediate solution to all the demons in my head. But I know it's a journey. And right now I am in my worst state for I even tried to end myself some time ago but my Sundhari saved me. But now I realize I should have brought her along on this journey. She would have loved all of you people. But I am not in a condition to even look after myself. How can I...' and my voice started breaking while tears ran from my eyes. But still, I continued to tell.

'How can I look after the person I wanna see for the rest of my life when I am like this? I have gone through so much that I want to get better but still, I wanna be there for her unconditionally...' and I started to weep silently. She gently wiped my tears reminding me of Mom.

'Suhana ma! Can I have a hug?'

'*Ah, ende mone. Vaa*!'(*Come here, my son*) and she hugged me while she said, 'Let it go!' as I cried onto her shoulders. The 3 girls and 2 boys(the children) who were staying in the home and studying in the nearby village also came around and hugged us. It sort of felt warm and consoling.

Suhana patted my back and assured me, '*Mone*! The greatest gift that you can give to others is the gift of unconditional love and acceptance. Subanallah, you will heal.'

Many months ago with Sundhari

I had prepared some rice, brinjal-potato fry, and some rasam as a comfort food since we both wanted to speak about something very crucial and we really might need such comfort. Since it was the beginning of the monsoons in Kerala, the rains were non-stop and the weather had been a bit colder too.

I heard her speaking while arriving at the corridor but I had to wait at the stove so rasam does not boil over. The timing of Rasam boiling over and the sound of her bell was in sync. Turning the burner off, and throwing a lid over the vessel, I ran to the door. She was literally yelling at someone and the entire apartment could hear her voice. I let her in and closed the door.

She was still arguing with her mom over the phone,

'Ma! I am just tired of this. I am tired of talking about this. You have one of the worst marriages I have seen. I am not going to take advice from you. I am very sorry to say. I am not in a hurry to get married and I guess I have lost count of how many times I have told this to you. No matter how many times you guilt trip me into a marriage, just because you want to look better in the eyes of the society and those relatives who barely give a shit about our pain — I can't. Yes, he may be a nice guy who lives in Texas or Bangalore or wherever corner of the world you say every time but that's not the only thing I see in someone. Many lack the ability to show emotions. I guess it should be quite obvious to you but you have never given ears to my words.'

'My timeline is not marrying someone when I am 26, bearing a child, doing sexual favours for a guy I know little about, and serving the house for all my life. Until I am confident, I can't marry someone. That too, the one I choose myself. Especially the one who understands me! Your plans can never be my plans, ma! Before you emotionally blackmail me for one more time, both of you sit down and talk and try to understand. Just think, maybe once from my shoes. And for the sake of goodness, stop hearing the words of some random guy who barely knows about me. Accept the fact! And don't message me or call me till tomorrow. I will not pick up. Bye, ma!'

She dropped her backpack on the floor and threw the phone across the hall. Luckily it landed on the bean bag.

'Kannama!' I said softly.

She came and hugged me. Sinking into me she said, 'Hmm! I wanted this Gautham! Sorry about the yelling in your apartment.'

Caressing her hair, I kissed her head and said, 'It's okay! You're okay.'

We stood there hugging silently without uttering a word, and after a minute passed by I could feel her becoming calm by the grip of her hands as they dropped towards my hips and her face dropping much more into my chest.

Sundhari said in a very low voice — 'Gautham! I'm so hungry, da. I did not eat since yesterday evening. Do you have something to eat?"

Wiping her tears, I told her — 'Yes, baby! Go wash your hands and come. I'll bring you a plate by then.'

As we sat together over lunch, it likely created a safe and understanding space for each other to express our feelings and struggles without judgment. She ate and felt so happy about having comfort food after a hard time with her family and also starving for a long time.

'Dei! This Rasam and Brinjal fry combo is kickass. Wow! You cook so good my man. Damn!'

'Do you want potato chips?'

'No no! This is fine. There's potato in this veggie fry.'

I booped her nose and said, 'You are my potato, my love!'

'Ayyeda! Always finding ways to say something like this. I love you too bro!'

We laughed about it and finished eating soon so we could rant about each other's lives. She spoke about her hardships since yesterday. Her parents wanted her to get married since when she was 22 but she had been fighting forever. Shedding a couple of tears out of anger and frustration during the entire conversation, I was waiting for her to finish it patiently.

After a small breath pause she said, 'Boy! You have been listening to me since I started yapping about my life. Say something no?'

I cleared my throat and started to speak.

'Baby! Your story about leaving a traumatic environment to focus on yourself and your career demonstrates your strength and resilience. You are a strong woman, my love. Making the decision to prioritize personal growth and well-being is commendable, and it even inspired me to see that positive change is possible, even after experiencing trauma.'

She kiddingly pinched my cheeks and smiled. A moment later she looked into my eyes and questioned, 'Gautham? Did you just...'

And I interrupted her with a YES.

'Do you wish to share?'

'I can try but I don't know.'

'Baby! I am here to listen. Try if you can but it's okay if you cannot continue. I can understand.'

For the next 15 minutes of trying hard to tell and taking so many pauses, shedding a couple of tears, and choking on my own words, I talked to her about the trauma and abuse in my childhood.

This entire conversation between the two of us likely involved a lot of active listening, empathy, and emotional support from both of us to each other. I had never in my life gathered the courage to tell this to anyone but she gave me assurance and encouragement, reminding me again that we accepted each other for who we were and what we had gone through, for good, for bad, and for neutral.

'My lovely Gautham! I wish you have all the strength you need and I am here if you need it. I know this is something you can never forget but I will help you with this journey as far as I can. This entire space between us is not only for romance, or fights, or anything as such but a safe space for such hard conversations.'

It was essential to acknowledge that discussing past traumas could be emotionally draining, and it was okay for both me and Sundhari to take breaks and practice self-care as we continued the healing journeys. 'Professional help, such as counselling or therapy, can also play a crucial role in processing and healing from past traumas,' she had said to me earlier. Overall, the lunch meeting likely strengthened our bond and we were left with a sense of solace and hope for the future.

'I love you da!'

'You are my seven wonders Sundhari!'

Episode #10

She's a TEN

B*ack in the Old age home, the current day*

The day after experiencing so many beautiful emotions, witnessing wonderful people, and hearing brilliant stories, Venba and I decided to leave by the morning after breakfast. Venba claimed suddenly that she did not want to extend her travel days. The woman I saw with such vigor and love for life, suddenly turned around.

Marudhu came with a small brown cover and handed it over to her. He informed, 'As Doctor Kani said, I have bought all the medicines she said. In case you need anything, I have informed them to give it to you. I will speak to them over the phone. Don't give them any money!'

The old man Kunjappan from the home came forward and asked Marudhu about it. They were talking about something and then the man walked towards her, 'Take care, Venba! The world may seem dangerous. But if you need anything, this home is here to take care of it.'

Venba — 'Thank you *acha*! We see the world as dangerous as it is, as precious as it is. To see beyond the inhibitions, the bricks we have built ourselves... to shake hands, hug, embrace, kiss, and importantly to feel... I think those things may be the purpose of my life. A life, with emotions.'

I was confused with the entire interaction and asked, 'Venba! Are you pregn..?!'

'HELLO!' — A man yelled down from the gate.

The gardener's son ran to the gate, spoke to him, and brought him inside. The man seemed to be wearing formal clothes but he had a small backpack stuffed probably with his clothes. He was a bit tired and panting due to the slopes of the estate.

Kunjappan asked, 'Hello! Namaskaram. How can we help you?'

He shook hands with him and said, 'My name is Ravi! I am... lost! from everything.'

Kunjappan looked at me and smirked then continued to speak with Ravi.

'You came to the right place! In fact, our friend Gautham can help you.'

I went speechless for a moment. It had been a very tough time and the people of the Home believed that I could be the strongest man ever. He gave me the responsibility of another person like me. With Venba in the mix, this was a deadly cocktail.

While Ravi was asked to freshen up and eat, Venba and I thought it would be better to tag him along on this journey. So we decided to stay till noon until he got food and rest. Everyone went on to do their work.

We went to the children's park area to sit on a swing. Venba came and sat on the swing next to me. We were slowly swinging. I looked at her while she was already looking at me.

'Venba! Why are you looking at me like that?'

'I was wondering Gautham! When are you going to ask me about the medicines you were so curious about?"

I stopped swinging and planted my feet on the ground. Some mud seeped into my toenails. 'That's your personal stuff, Venba!'

'Gautham! When I am about to tell a story, you listen. Don't dismiss it!'

She continued — 'It's something about me and my journey. I thought that I was safe, but it turns out that isn't the case. No one can be too safe you see and in the hands of fate, I have a life in my hands.'

It seemed she was going to reveal something to me. She was a little disappointed to say something but the information was not the most disappointing thing to happen to a person. Maybe she was pregnant? So I asked her again if she was.

She had a short bellyful laugh.

'No Gautham! It's sometimes, the time that isn't trying to grow with you. I don't. I am very much safe on that part you see.'

I was getting flummoxed as her reactions gave me mixed feelings. Venba was happy and accepting of the truths she had. 'Venba! It doesn't make sense. You said you have to meet your mom because her time is less. And now you're here with medicines. And you want to cut short your journey. Is she alright? Something wrong? Should we visit her first? Can you please get to the point? It's like Rachel's 18-page letter.'

Chuckling softly, Venba looked at me — 'Yeah, I told you there's less time! But it isn't for her that I was talking about. And the medicines are not for my mother. I thought I'd get one last chance to see my mom before fate eats me up. Gautham, I have cancer. And there's no way it can be treated fully.'

Contd... — Some months ago after Lunch at Gautham's place

Overall, this lunch meeting likely strengthened our bond and we were left with a sense of solace and hope for the future.

'I love you da!'

'You are my seven wonders Sundhari!'

She blushed as she held her cheeks and asked if she could lie down on the sofa. I obliged and tried to get up. She hit my hand and said, 'Sit your ass down, mister.' And she rested her head on my lap and took my hand to keep on her head. Slowly caressing her hair, she closed her eyes and said — 'Baby! Remember our first time when we..'

'Yeah, I remember that. Our first fight itself was so crazy. I thought you were wrestling me and going to pin me down.'

'Yeah, I did pin you down!' And she giggled naughtily.

'Hey! What are you talking about?'

She opened her eyes to side-eye me and chuckled, 'Turn on that tube light. It will turn on faster than you.'

'Ayy! Yeah, I do remember that day. It was also lunchtime.'

Rewind to the day when they fought!

Sundhari arrived at my entrance and it was very evident when she knocked it more loudly than usual.

'Coming!'

Opening the door, she stormed in while piercing me with her eyes. I closed the door and asked her to come to my room to have the conversation.

'Da!'

'Sundhari wait! People in this apartment can hear us. At least let's not disturb them. We will talk in my room, come!'

'Yeah, yeah! Now you are aware of everything huh?' She went to my room keeping her bag near the TV stand.

I walked into my room and saw her sitting on the bed, hands crossed and with literally nose-smoking anger.

'Sundhari! I have been trying so much. It is not like I never wanted to take a step but trying now is going to take a lot of stuff.'

'Gautham! I am not trying to enforce anything. Did I ever say that you have to do this? I have been laying out the facts. It may push your goals a year or two later. No one is going to chase you for that. I have seen you solve problems with so much ease and the way your face lights up when you pick up an Advanced Physics book. And why do you think I brought you that puzzle last month because you are nerdy? No, it is to encourage you to do something for yourself.'

I exhaled loud and asked her, 'Sundhari! It has been so traumatic when I did this before. I am tired of these arguments. You know how much I loved Science ever since my childhood and because I did not stand up for myself, I lost so much and I am working as a Senior Business Analyst because at least I can sit and forget about what I loved.'

She stood up, rushed towards me and grabbed my T-shirt. She pulled me closer and said while her volume gradually increased, "I am not fighting. Can't you see? I saw how much you prepped for the exams. Now you got a seat in the college that you could only dream of, and it has also offered you a scholarship and industrial exposure. So, you're being paid to study and work. Why are you backing out now?'

'That University offered me because the dad who barely cared for me all these years is looking to feel awesome among his colleagues that his son is studying in the same college where he works as some Department Head.'

Her grip loosened. She went a step back and her eyes gleamed. 'I am sorry! Why did you not tell me?'

'Because I didn't wanna leave a person like you just to go and live a life I dreamed of, but hate to this very minute that I did. This dream may not work this way.'

The energy of us slowing down, she asked me the same question again. I explained to her my tragic and idiotic backstory. I spoke about how much I was passionate and then talked to her about the medals I had gotten for the experiments in college.

She assured me that she'd contribute as much as she could. Sundhari had a way of articulating things in a very poetic way sometimes. She said,

"Neerum, nizhalum pola neenda arul udaiya oorire!

ennai uya konmin, poril pugalum kali yaanai Sundhari kodhai Gauthamanukku

Azhalum en nenjam kidandhu!"

(Oh! The citizens of the town who are greatly gracious like water and shade,

Please save me!

My love for Gautham! A king who took my heart,

who owns elephants and wins battles, is lying in my heart and scorching it)

I was awestruck!

With time, the conversation shifted from blaming myself to a more understanding and empathetic tone. Sundhari acknowledged my feelings, and I, in turn, listened to her about how much she was there to support me. Slowly, the walls of anger and defensiveness started to crumble and were replaced by a growing desire to find a resolution.

Many minutes later, there was silence. I took her hand in mine and said, 'I promise that I will talk to you whatever it is. I'll never allow this miscommunication or misunderstanding to escalate to arguments again. You are my inspiration. My lightning rod! You keep me grounded.'

She stood up and came in front of me, raised her hand, and pointed her index finger at my face, 'Look if you don't say something I will understand. It's okay, my love. But if you make one more science joke, I dunno what I'm gonna do.'

'Hey! I was just making a Lightning logic. Don't pass your current on to me.'

She smiled and pushed me to the bed. Supporting her one hand on my chest and one hand on the bed, she sat over me. She kept her index finger on my mouth trying to shush me, then said — 'We'll see which current is stronger.'

She kept her hands on either side of my head and came closer. She looked into my eyes and whispered, 'Gautham!'

'Sundhari!'

And then we kissed! We made out like a mess.

Sundhari - 'Dude! Gentle.'

I stuttered, 'Urm!!! You're the one who bit my lips. Don't you tell me to be gentle!'

Sundhari suddenly grabbed my hair and pulled my head away. 'Eda! Are you protected?'

I gave her a naughty smirk and winked, 'Present and accounted for!'

Grabbing me by my neck and pulling me close, she bit her teeth to say - 'Suit up, man'

I swiftly ran into the bathroom and came out in my boxers showing her a thumbs-up. She was, in the meantime, making herself comfortable. I was asking her so many questions to make sure she was okay.

At some point, I annoyingly asked her again when she was already okay with it and then she shut my mouth with her hands and said, 'I want this mouth of yours to do something else than talking.'

Almost an hour later, we cuddled and she said okay to my long pending request to her. She let me be her small spoon while cuddling. Then we took a nap.

Episode #11

E-LE-VEN-OP

At the old age home, the current day

After hearing the most devastating news from Venba that she had cancer, I couldn't react in any way. The nights I thought of ending myself, she had endured too. But it was in a different painful way. With a heavy heart, I started the car, while Ravi sat in the back and Venba in the passenger seat.

We were descending the hill by afternoon and since it was the monsoon season, we were lucky that we missed getting toasted in the sun. The afternoon was dark, gloomy, and moody, just like my mind.

Ravi started to speak — 'Gautham! I heard that you were travelling with no destination in mind. Would it be okay if I could accompany you? All along!'

Venba looked at him with surprise and said, 'I hope he agrees. It's good to have company. Right, Gautham?'

I shook my head for which she tapped my head gently, 'Gautham! Just because I told you about me, doesn't mean you have to be like that. You have your own struggles. This is mine! And mine alone. Just drive dude!'

Ravi started to talk. He had been a man of so much black and white. He had been living a high life and even was the father of a teenager. Ravi should at least be 45 years old. But the entire dysfunction finally broke him. He said, 'You know, my company never let me go although I always wanted to become a professor. I just want to do something creative and my work eats up most of my time. Well, looking from the other side, I'd sleep better at the office because the family has never been so kind because I rebelled a lot when I was young. I had a brother but he was too distant, my kid was close to me but since my wife and I are not on good terms, that's a bit rough too. We spoke about separation also but nothing official. And now that he's a teenager, we all know how much we hated our dad at that point in our lives. No matter how hard you try, just doesn't sit well. I wasn't so pushy or did things because I'd get a name. No! Yeah, whatever man. Sorry about that.'

Venba took a peek at Ravi and switched off the Spotify that was playing in the car.

'Ravi! As probably the most messed up person in the car, I can tell you just one thing – I can sense how hard you must be feeling about your life. It is so tough, but I wish it gets better for you. Whatever decision you pick, let it only give you peace.'

Ravi — 'Yeah. Thank you, Venba, for saying that. It's just no one has ever told me that except I figured out a way for myself. After seeing all this, I went on to fix myself. I went for counselling and found the way for myself. I just wanted one break out of all this, you know. I wrote on a piece of paper that I wanted a break and now I am here. With two people who took me in more than my family ever did in the last few years.'

While I could speak something back, my phone rang after a while.

Venba — 'What if it's her?'

I chuckled, 'Wouldn't be! She knows me. She probably hates me now!' and I peeked to see it was my sister. I pulled over to the side of the road where the view of the valley was fantastic in this climate. A slight yellow ray of sunset broke through the clouds hitting the wet trees of the valley among the mountains.

Ravi was amazed to see that I was still using my flip phone instead of a smartphone as a main device.

'Hello Tara! Gautham speaking.'

Venba signalled to put it on speaker. I reluctantly turned on the speaker and she said 'hi' too.

Tara — 'Hi! I'm Tara. Who am I talking to now?'

Venba — 'Hello Tara! I am Venba. Just a fellow traveller. Just wanted to say hi to you.'

Tara — 'Nice to talk to you Ms. Venba! Gautham! There is something important I wanna say da.'

Me — 'Tell me.'

Tara — 'Sundhari called me in the morning. She was holding up ok but it shook me when she said what you did. I'm not gonna tell you to go back or something like that. I know you did it for yourself. She told me to just convey one thing. Actually, she sent me an image. It was a letter but she also informed that you're using a flip phone. First of all, are you a caveman? And second, what the actual fuck? Can you at least tell me if you have your laptop with you?"

I chuckled — 'No Tara! I don't.'

'Why are you like this?'

Venba intervened — 'Tara! You can send it to me.'

Tara paused and said, 'Can I have your number?'

After saving her number, Tara immediately forwarded it to Venba and Venba thanked her. I sarcastically mentioned, 'Tara! Venba is single, just in case.'

Tara — 'Venba, ignore him. Bye! I'll text you tomorrow.'

As I cut the call, I started the car. Venba kept looking at me, and then she asked me in a calm voice, 'How long are you going to distance yourself like this? Don't you want to read the letter?'

'Can you read it for me?'

The letter goes —

Gautham,

My love! I hope the world is treating you better. For me, it is a little bit ok. But not so much without your presence. I love you. I want you to know that even though I miss you terribly, I am finding the strength to cope with the distance between us. Each day that passes, I yearn about the day when we can finally reunite, both healed and stronger than ever. While the pain of your absence remains, I want you to understand that I am carrying our love in my heart as a source of comfort.

Your love has become my guiding light, helping me navigate through the challenges and uncertainties that life would present. I draw strength from the memories we've created and the bond we share, knowing that they will sustain me until the day we can be together again.

If I have caused you any pain, I am very sorry. I understand why you want to stay away from everyone you know. Your journey towards healing is my priority too, and I want you to focus on that with all your might. I have faith that time will work its magic, bringing us back together when the moment is right.

Abracadabra! (In case Time's magic needs my support, I also put my spell)

I am not mad at you for going alone. The thought of your smile, though distant, brings warmth to my heart. Gautham, please take care of yourself. Focus on your healing, your growth, and your well-being.

And I'd choose you; in a hundred lifetimes, in a hundred thousand worlds, in any different reality, after any canon events, I'd find you and I'd choose you. You are a work of art. An art I admire and may never get tired of.

I look forward to your words anytime you wish to say. Thank you for teaching me to write letters.

With so much love,

Yours.

Some months before at Gautham-Sundhari home

As Sundhari was finishing up her meetings by 5:30, she also was waiting for Gautham to arrive home from his therapy session after lunch.

She put up his favourite '70s English rock songs over the speakers. The calling bell rang. She ran to the door to receive him. His face seemed content. His eyes gleamed with peace.

'Sundhari!' he greeted her and they walked in. He closed the door behind him and hugged her tightly. There were some moments of silence and peace.

He softly spoke, 'You put on my favourite music. It's Mellifluous!'

'Because Gautham, you are a Seraphic. You deserve good music.'

He planted a gentle kiss on her forehead and said, 'You are a work of art. An art I admire and will never get tired of.'

She went to get him the juice she prepared.

Gautham smiling, crossed the room to her. 'It was... surprisingly liberating. My therapist helped me sift through some of the memories I've been carrying like weight. I feel like a burden has been lifted. Temporarily at least.'

Sundhari standing, stepped closer to him, 'I'm so glad to hear that, Gautham. You deserve all the happiness and light in the world.'

Gautham placed his hand on her cheek, 'You've been my light, Sundhari. Your unwavering support and love have been my anchor through these turbulent times.'

Sundhari placing her hand over his said, 'And you, my dear Gautham, have shown me strength in vulnerability. Your willingness to confront your past and heal inspires me every day.'

Led Zeppelin's Stairway to Heaven started to play in the background.

Gautham pulled her into his arms, their bodies fitting perfectly as if they were two pieces of a puzzle meant to be together. They sway gently to the music, their movements guided by an invisible hand, a dance of intimacy and connection.

Their dance slowed, and Gautham tilted Sundhari's chin upward, capturing her lips in a kiss that spoke volumes about their love, the battles they've fought and the promises they've made.

Gautham pulled back slightly, his forehead against hers, 'You're the best!'

Sundhari her eyes shimmering with tears that refused to roll down her cheeks, 'And you are my best!'

In unison, they said — 'For the next Nine Hundred and Ninety-Nine Lives!'

Episode #12

and the clock struck TWELVE

TWO MONTHS LATER at home with Sundhari and her brother

The sister and brother were watching *Zindagi na milegi dobara* at her home while she was constantly laughing when the Moshi-Moshi scene came up. She rewound the entire scene to watch it again.

Sundhari has seen this movie so many times already, and every time she felt like travelling but she did not.

It had already been more than 2 months since Gautham had left. While the scene was playing on TV for the second time, Sundhari's face became emotionless. Her brother slowly noticed her face — the tears from her left eye were waiting to fall down her cheeks. He used to call her Suna since childhood.

As they sat on the bean bags, he pulled her beanbag towards him and asked, 'Suna! What happened?'

Switching off the TV, she kept the remote on the snack table before them. She took a sip of cold coffee that Achuthan made and spoke, 'Achu! I just feel like a tree. Like a beautiful song bird had sat on me singing the tune of his, and it flew away in its journey of a long mile. The tree yearns for the bird that sang on it. The tree that yearns to fly away with it. Thinking that it would return. You understand?'

Achuthan cleared his throat, put his arm forward and caressed her head, 'Yes!'

Wiping her tears, she sipped from her coffee mug and continued her analogy — 'You know he had left me back here with just one letter. I sent him mine as a response and still, he hasn't written back. What happens to the love I radiated for him? Where does this leave me now? What would you do if you were in my place?'

Achuthan smiled and said, 'Suna! First of all, two people speaking over the letter at this age is wonderful. But, I understand that you tend to dwell on the moments you could have shared, more times than the moments you both lived through. You know why exactly he left. You of all people, understand that!'

Sundhari had finished her coffee by the time Achuthan finished talking — 'Alright then Achu! It's fine I guess! Because he has been fighting all his life till now and when I met him, it was still the same. It was still his fight but maybe I joined him to fight together for each other. He knew letting his guard down to let me in to love each other from all sides through thick and thin, was indeed okay. We even spoke about that. But somehow he ventured out to find himself! If that's what he thinks would work, then so be it.'

He nodded.

A moment of silence later, he spoke — 'Do something as I say! Close your eyes. Don't speak until I ask you to,' and as she did, he continued, 'Take a deep breath and exhale... Take another one and think of a beautiful sunset time on your balcony.

You are standing with him. So closely! He looks at you while the orange rays of sunlight hit you both. A mild breeze brings warmth to your heart. Now! You look at him. You tell him something. It can be a story, a proposal, you could even scold him. Say what you want to him.'

She elicited a poetic dialogue—

'Budhdhu! Can I kiss and heal your wound? If it is possible, I would not be able to kiss your heart. So, I'd kiss your neck, your hands, your forehead, your cheeks, your lips. Hoping they seep in and reach your heart. Your life may seem full of struggles and scribbles. But you are the artwork that I love. Even an art gallery could not be as unique as you. I would draw on you with my hands, photograph you with my eyes, or just sit and stare at you, reminding myself that your effort to become such a work is one I could learn from.'

Achuthan took a moment to see if she wanted to continue.

The silence struck her again. He said, 'Good. Now, slowly open your eyes. Come back to this moment. Tell me what you feel.'

She began to bawl and fell onto Achuthan's beanbag to hug her brother. Sundhari uncontrollably cried out loud for a long time while Achuthan consoled her.

'Wait for him, little one!'

With a shrill tone, she replied — '*WHY, CHETA?*' *(why, brother?)*

Achuthan replied calmingly — 'Because that's what people do when they are in love. They wait!'

'Thank you, Achu!' sniffled and continued - 'I remember this one time we spent a day together, Achu. He was back from his bike trip with his friends. I invited him home the next day.' She chuckled and blushed. 'It was a fun day da Achu!' Achuthan tapped her head and stepped to the balcony to pick up a call he received.

She sank into the beanbag reminiscing about that day and began smiling.

<u>*A few months ago when they were dating*</u>

Sunday dawned with the promise of a leisurely day, and Gautham, feeling the warmth of the morning sun, found himself awake from his slumber at 9 AM. As he lazily stretched and contemplated the day ahead, a message from Sundhari, popped up on his phone.

She invited him to spend the day at her home, and without hesitation, he rang her.

Gautham - 'Good morning Ms. Sunshine!'

Sundhari - 'It's 9 AM asshole! Get ready and come home as soon as you can. Take a bath and come. Then I have a few veggies. Can you get it for me when you come?'

Gautham - 'Ehn?'

She started to say again and he interrupted, 'Haan, okay kannama!'

She laughed and said - 'Kalla! Alright, see you here.'

Within an hour and a half, Gautham found himself standing at Sundhari's doorstep, greeted by her infectious smile. Eager to make the most of their time together, they embarked on a day filled with shared moments and unbridled joy.

Seeing him after quite a while, she welcomed him with a hug.

"My teddy bear!" she said, tightening her grasp around his hips. A moment later, Gautham kissed her head and she pinched his hips and giggled.

The house is filled with their laughs now.

He went to keep the vegetables in the refrigerator and after arranging everything he asked, 'You got no snacks?'

Sundhari entered the kitchen and wolf-whistled at him. 'I see one; staring into the fridge!'

Biting his teeth to control laughter, he opened the freezer, dispensed the ice tray and ate an ice cube. She swiftly came to close the fridge door, grabbed him by his sweatshirt, and pulled him close.

'Don't you freaking bite that ice cube!' and they kissed. A few sloppy seconds later, she successfully took the ice cube into her mouth and bit it.

Gautham's breathing was elevated for obvious reasons. He opened the freezer again and put one ice cube on top of his head for which Sundhari laughed and laughed until her stomach hurt.

Gautham - 'Why are you laughing?'

Sundhari - 'It's so funny to see you like this. You make me laugh so much.'

They had all the time for themselves at her home. Beginning to cook, she cut the tomatoes and onions. She then blanched some cauliflower while Gautham prepped to make a Cauliflower65 and kneaded the dough for chapatis.

She walked near, took some flour in her hand, threw it onto his face and ran outside the kitchen while he choked and sneezed. He wiped and patted off the flour from his eyes and ran to her, while she put on the hoodie which he wore.

'Hey! That's my comfy hoodie.'

'Sounds about right, Budhdhu!'

With a fake growl in his voice, Gautham spoke - 'I'll end up having no shirts to wear.'

'Okay, that.... That sounds tasty.'

Blushing with atta flour on his face, he said 'Okay, stop making me blush. I need to cook.'

Cooking together, they spoke a lot about their favourite dishes, including the ones their mothers cooked. Finally an hour later, with chapatis, paneer butter masala and cauliflower 65, their tummies were fulfilled.

Sundhari finally let go of his hoodie but she went straight into her room and kept it away from her boyfriend's reach. She came back into the hall to see him sitting on the sofa, legs up, doing something on his phone. She whistled looking at him.

'Come to Mama!' she said and crawled onto him. He kept his phone on the floor nearby and caressed her hair while she laid her head on his chest.

'Shall you not let go of me for some more time?' he asked.

'Your wish is granted, my boyfriend!' she pinched him gently. He put one arm around her back and another hand cupping her face, his thumb slowly stroking her cheeks.

A few silent minutes passed by. She lifted her head towards his face and asked, 'Can I ask you something, baby?'

He nodded with no inhibitions in his face or mind. For the first time, he was not afraid of the question. Every time he got close, someone or something let go of him which made him ask that question.

Such thoughts had made him assume that he was becoming intrusive in everyone's lives.

'I know we haven't said this to each other more than once. Why?'

Gautham smiled - 'Our actions said it a lot of times to each other. Wearing my hoodie, cooking you food, making me breakfast when I was sick and even laying your head on my chest and slowing down my heart rate. We've said to each other many times indirectly.'

She supported one hand on the sofa and sat on him. While he also sat up, she put one leg towards his side and the other leg hung down. Sitting on his thighs, she pulled herself closer to him.

She pulled his hands and placed them onto her hips. She cupped her palms onto his face and that action made his hands tighter on her hips. She naughtily smiled.

Sundhari closed her eyes, inhaled, opened them, exhaled and looked straight into his eyes. The souls met. He mentioned that her eyes pierced him.

Sundhari uttered, 'I love you!' and smiled.

Gautham softly murmured, 'I love you!' and a tear rolled down his left eye, while his right eyes pooled.

Her hands were still over his cheeks not wiping off the tears. She waited for him to express it all. Gautham's lips trembled, face twitched, and he was almost about to cry.

'I have never been held this way!' he said.

Her warm smile consoled him and as she nodded, he said, 'I love you!'

And now she wiped the tears off his face with her thumbs while still holding his face, she replied, 'You deserve this, Gautham! You are loved!'

She went forward and put her forehead against his forehead. Their noses booped. Her hands were around his shoulder and his hands were wrapped around her hip.

He whispered - 'We never realize how frozen we are, until someone breaks that ice off!'

The gap between their bodies decreased and to ensure it, she wrapped her legs around him and they sunk into each other in a hug. Their faces stuck to each other. His tears stopped and his heart calmed down again. Rubbing each other's cheeks at first, he initiated a kiss now. Locking eye contact at first, the faces came towards each other.

A minute and a half passed by. Sundhari spoke, 'Trust the magic! You are a wizard now, Harry!'

Episode #13

B, Yaavarum Nalam

C*urrently in Kashmir, Gautham tells us his story*.

We stayed in a hotel called Vivanta Dal View which overlooked the partly frozen Dal Lake and the backdrop was these magnificent snow-covered mountains.

I was writing my daily gratitude journal sitting on the bed while Ravi sat on the balcony enjoying the light at 3 p.m. with a chai he ordered.

'How's the Chai, Mr. Ravi?'

Ravi said loudly, 'With this weather with no sun in the afternoon along with this fantastic snowfall, it's just brilliant!'

A few seconds later, 'Gautham! Is that Venba in the garden by the pool? Why is she standing during the snowfall? Come look at this bro!'

I ran to the balcony and saw her standing.

'Let's go check on her!'

We wore our coats, and shoes and reached the garden.

Ravi said in a loud voice while in the garden, 'Waiting to propose to someone Venba?'

She was silent and still looking at the mountains. We knew something was not right. We slowly went near and just stood with her. She gave me a packet of cashews and said, 'Some kid found me standing here, gave me this and ran away. You take it!'

A minute later I looked at Venba — 'How are you Venba?'

And immediately her face changed. Maybe I should not have asked that question.

A few weeks ago in her hometown

While we got down from the hills where the old-age home was situated, we took the route straight to her home in

Telangana. We just stopped for food and sleep. Most of the time, Ravi and I took turns and drove because of one reason.

Venba seemed to experience pain in her stomach and she thought, her medicines were going to give up on her. She called her doctor to ask and she was advised for a scan. While on our way, we stopped at Coimbatore to get it done. She got the results the same day, but the news was much worse from her doctor.

Her tumours had worsened a little more than before and now she was being recommended to get more blood work. She might also need chemotherapy within a month. Her life took a U-turn while she had to digest this fact. We stayed in a hotel for almost 2 weeks for her preliminary treatments and tests.

Her mother who had been a diabetic for many years experienced a heart attack when she heard such a piece of bad news. What parent would feel fine if they knew that their child was having cancer and had only a few more days to live? But this was much worse. We didn't know all these days since we met that she hadn't told her mother about her condition fully. Unable to handle the shock, her mother got a massive heart attack.

We finally reached her hometown after Venba's tests were completed and went straight to the hospital where the mother was admitted. It was quite a long month. We stopped for two days in Bangalore since the car had to be serviced for repairs due to overheating.

Days passed by very quickly. We tried our best to manage money throughout the trip and although I had been paying for the fuel, Ravi took care of all the other expenses. He made us eat good food and stay in decent hotels.

Venba knew with her tumour's condition, it could be the last time she would visit her mother. But little did she know, that it could be so devastatingly true for both.

We reached her mother's home and while Venba spent time in the bedroom near her mother, Ravi and I tried to cook for all of us.

Venba was talking to her mom, and she excused herself to come see us in the kitchen before lunchtime. Suddenly there was a noise coming from the bedroom. We rushed!

Venba's mother was lying unconscious. With the help of a neighbour, we contacted a final-year MBBS student in the same locality. He rushed to the house and checked on her mother. No signs of luck! Or Life.

Minutes later, the doctor arrived from a nearby hospital and confirmed it too.

Venba didn't shed a tear and right after her mother's cremation, she asked if she could accompany me on the journey.

Ravi – 'Don't you want to stay here? Your people are here.'

Venba – 'No Ravi! You know yesterday morning she was talking to me about her trip to the Himalayas with my dad when they got married. Maybe I can take her there. She'd like to rest among the mountains.'

<u>*Back to Kashmir*</u>

She wanted to hug, and then Ravi and I hugged her. This group hug seemed to comfort her in pain. Venba finally cried and said, 'Thank you guys! I wouldn't know it would be this comforting to have brothers. I could never forget you both. You guys are my yellow!'

Letting go of the hug after 2 minutes, we were covered in snow and Ravi's head caught more snow due to his coily-curl hair.

Venba began laughing at him with tears in her eyes while she looked at him. I immediately took a picture of him. The poor guy did not know what was happening. Ravi also started laughing looking at the photo.

We walked towards the other end of the garden and stopped to look at some children playing in the park while it snowed. Priya called out to us in an exhilarating voice, "Guys! Goddamn. There you are! I got lost when I went out for a walk and luckily this hotel cab driver was on his way to pick up someone. So I hitched a ride in his car and came. I left my phone back in the room to charge it. By the way, I saw a greenhouse that way, which also seems to be a butterfly garden. We should go there. The weather inside is surprising! Also, we need to see the Drung Waterfall which stays frozen in this weather. Did you know a fact about that frozen waterf..."

Ravi interrupted her — 'Priya! Slow down!'

She replied with a chuckle, 'Guys! I am so used to talking and for a moment I thought I was on a trek. Sorry! Anyway, what's up?'

Oh yeah! Meet Priya from Delhi. Or at least we met her there. She was a trek leader by profession and she joined us at the hotel we stopped by to have our dinner. Taking so many people on a journey of their lifetime, she decided to take some time off and go someplace without an itinerary. Guess with whom she got stuck. Of course, us! She let us park the car in her Trek Organization's office and booked us all a flight to Srinagar.

I told her, 'We were just talking in the garden area by the lamps.'

Priya took Venba's hand and kept it between hers like a sandwich. She patted her hands and said, 'We're with you!'

Venba – 'Thank you, Priya.'

Priya asked, 'Venba! Do you want to say something to your mom? I am sure she's listening from somewhere.'

While Priya still held hands, Ravi and I stood close to her. Venba looked at the snow-covered mountains and wiped her eyes off the tears. We looked too! I mean, who can let go of their eyes looking at such a beautiful scene?

I began noticing beauty in nature again after a long time. Sundhari used to tell me to romanticize such moments.

Venba spoke —

'Ma! You always loved these mountains! Maybe if you are there, hear me out. Nothing has been the same since you left. The odds were always against me, but you didn't want me to fixate on them. Well, here's a catch. I always did. I am filling in the blanks of the memories we never made. I wish it turned out differently 'cause you always told me to believe in the impossible. You were an amazing dancer. We could've danced to just one song before you drifted away. I will miss you ma! And I love you!'

Episode #14

Like a February FOURTEEN

By evening, they gathered at the hotel's café, sipping on hot coffees and taking in the stunning view of the snow-capped mountains in the distance through the massive windows. As they chatted and enjoyed their morning beverages, Priya's excitement was palpable. She couldn't contain her enthusiasm about a nearby greenhouse that also housed a butterfly park. Her animated stories about lush greenery and colourful butterflies sparked the interest of the group. She was hyping them about butterflies and Ravi said, 'I thought it was a marketing gimmick but honestly, I feel this is legit. Sometimes we get to places while lost.'

Gautham replied, 'Life lessons eh?! Yeah, we do.'

For Gautham, adventure was never far from his mind, and Priya's description of this unique attraction was enough to pique his curiosity. The thought of exploring a greenhouse butterfly park amidst the cold and snowy surroundings of Kashmir sounded like a fantastic way to spend the day.

Turning to the others with a smile, Venba agreed, 'Come on guys! It sounds like a fantastic experience. Let's go.'

Priya immediately called the driver over a phone call. They eagerly hopped into the car, excited about the journey that lay ahead.

The drive itself was a memorable experience. They passed through idyllic landscapes, with fields of snow which would be colourful flowers, and quaint villages dotting the countryside. The beauty of Kashmir never ceased to amaze them, and the journey to the greenhouse was a journey through paradise.

Venba — 'You walked all this way, Priya? We've been driving for almost 20 minutes now.'

Priya sarcastically opened her hands and said, 'Excuse me, ma'am! But I've been gone for 2 hours since lunch.'

Upon reaching their destination, these newfound friends were greeted by a scene of serenity. The greenhouse was a lush haven, filled with exotic plants from different corners of the world. Butterflies, in a kaleidoscope of colours, danced through the air, their wings catching the feeble sunlight filtering through the glass walls.

They strolled through the winding paths, marvelling at the beauty of the butterflies and the vibrant blooms. Some of the more curious butterflies even landed gently on their hands and shoulders, creating a connection between humans and nature that was so heartwarming.

As they explored the greenhouse, they discovered the fascinating life cycle of the butterflies, from delicate eggs to eerie-looking caterpillars, mysterious chrysalises, and finally, the emergence of exquisite butterflies.

After an hour of exploration, they were reluctant to leave the butterfly park, their hearts filled with gratitude for the beautiful experience they had shared. It was also quite warm inside which was much better than the nose-cracking chills outside.

As the sun began its descent behind the majestic mountains of Kashmir, Gautham couldn't help but feel a deep sense of contentment. The visit to the greenhouse butterfly park had not only been his day of adventure but also a day of bonding and creating cherished memories with newfound friends. It was a perfect chapter in his journey through this picturesque region, and Gautham knew that the magic of Kashmir would stay with them forever.

One among the people in charge of the well-being of the butterflies, Mr. Vaasil asked Gautham if he wanted to walk into the caged portion of the greenhouse which housed rare Purple Emperor butterflies and Blue Morpho Butterflies. He realized Venba had requested him to permit Gautham.

Vaasil and Gautham walked inside the cage and closed the grill mess gate behind them. Vaasil asked Gautham to slowly raise his hands and point towards its legs. The blue morpho butterfly almost as big as his palm hesitated, then slowly walked onto his hands. The entire group was taking videos and photos of this cute moment. Vaasil smiled and shook his head.

Venba softly spoke, 'Months of rollercoaster. You are having your butterfly effect now.'

Admiring the slow movements of the Morpho, Gautham was fascinated by the feeble tickling on his hand. A calm surrounded him and inside him.

A gate noise from near the entrance.

Startled by the sound, the Morpho butterfly fluttered in his palm and flew towards his face. It sat on his nose and started to slowly move its wings.

Vaasil whispered, 'Sir! Don't breathe heavily. I will take a picture.' He took a fantastic portrait of Gautham smiling at the ticklish butterfly on his face.

Gautham — 'Venba! A Butterfly landed on my face.' His eyes welled up with tears.

A voice from behind the cage near a small tree called out, "Gautham!"

As the butterfly flew and sat on the flower tree's branches, he looked around, walked outside the cage, and strutted towards the tree, 'Maara?'

5 days before: in their home while Sundhari was being consoled by her brother

The door-phone rang from the security downstairs. She quickly stood up and walked fast and picked up the phone.

A small noise and then the security spoke, 'Hello, Ms. Sundhari!'

'Yes, Cheta. What is it?'

Security — 'One gentleman has come and he's refusing to show his ID card saying he has come from Visakhapatnam. Do you know this person? Could you please come here to avoid the confusion?'

'Yes. I'm coming there in 2 minutes. Ask him to wait!'

She kept the phone and looked at her brother with a question in her mind.

'Would it be him?' She then said, 'It was the security. Someone is at the gate with no ID card asking for me.'

'Come, let's go,' he said and they rushed towards the lift.

They reached the security cabin and the man said, 'Hello ma'am! I have not seen this man here. He's so colourful and has such a good sense of humour.'

The person was sitting inside the cabin and the security called out to him via the window.

Sundhari had high hopes that it would be Gautham but since the security described him differently, she confirmed it wasn't him.

The man came out with a rucksack-backpack and said in a bright tone, 'Hello! You are Sundhari, right? Come! Now we can go.'

Sundhari — 'Who are you? How do you know me?'

Achuthan took a few steps towards him. The man immediately laughed and said, 'Brother! Don't panic. Sundhari! I came to know you through Gautham. I had the privilege to travel with him for a couple of days. I am here to take you to him. Currently, I have heard he is on his way to Kashmir.' He showed a group selfie of Gautham, Ravi, Venba, and Priya inside a car.

He also showed a video of Venba. Initially, the video showed Gautham sleeping in the car while Priya and Venba had planned out this entire thing. The video was her talking in a lower voice, '*Hi Sundhari! My name is Venba. I am a fellow traveller of Gautham! I am sure you miss him. He talks in his sleep. And while on our way he had once mentioned that you wanted to come along but he left you back there. Guess what! He even once said it was a bad idea to leave you behind. I had some difficult times like this so I decided that I would do everything in my power to make it happen. We are on our way to Delhi airport. I will ask the man who's standing in front of you to bring you here. His name is Charlie! I can vouch for him. Please talk to him. He is to be trusted. Gautham misses you so much! If you wish to come, please do. You are the one.*'

Gautham's loud voice from behind — 'Sundhari!'

She stopped talking since Gautham had woken up from a dream. The video frame was pointing somewhere but she could hear him talking. It was not audible clearly but Sundhari could hear him say that he had a bad dream. The video ended with Venba showing a thumbs-up.

The man took his phone from her hands and said, 'If you trust me, you can come. Or else, I can give Venba's number and the place they are going. You can go see him by yourself. We all friends would love to see you both together, Sundhari. I'll wait by this handsome security chettan. Take your time and tell me your decision.'

Achuthan immediately answered, 'You got a place for one more person? I have never seen Kashmir.'

Sundhari was still processing everything. She couldn't react and was emotionless. Achuthan felt a little shine of hope on her face and understood she wanted to go see him.

She said to her brother, 'He won't hate me, no?'

Achuthan hugged her sideways by the shoulder and replied, 'He will not. He loves you, my little one! And by the way, I totally have to stay back because of my work. New clients for the Interior works. You are gonna be fine!' Sundhari turned again towards the messenger and asked, 'You are doing so much for us. What's your name again?'

He raised his hand forward for a handshake.

'Charlie!'

Episode #15

FIFTEEN second of Joy

A *t the Butterfly Park*

I exclaimed to Venba, 'Venba! A Butterfly landed on my face' and I literally felt like crying. I mentally counted from one and when I counted to fifteen, a voice beyond the cage near a small tree called out, 'Gautham!'

As I saw someone walk towards me, the butterflies that were sitting on me, flew back to the plants, flowers, and trees inside the enclosure. We came out and Vaasil closed the cage.

Ah, it was a familiar face from Varkala cafe. 'Maara?'

Maara — 'Hey!'

Venba immediately said, 'Oh! Hi! You must be the guy. Let us go to our hotel and speak. We'll run out of time, Manimaara!'

I asked, 'Wait, you know Maaran?'

Priya held her wrist and asked in a studious voice — 'What's running out?'

Maaran replied with a smile, 'Time!'

We wore our coats and walked outside. It was such a contrast as the chill wind hit our faces like a thousand needles. Ravi was stuttering to speak due to the cold.

He almost bit his tongue while he uttered, 'Arr car!? Sawwvy. Cha! Sorry. Where is our car?'

Maaran brightly laughed, 'Sir! I have a Jeep. Come on! ' He joyfully put his hand around Ravi's shoulders and walked along.

Maaran drove all the way to our hotel. He greeted the welcome staff as if he knew them well. Turns out, he now owned that Jeep. He said that he helped out a retired Lieutenant Colonel in the Army from Jharkhand and the old gentleman who owned this classic piece of vehicle gave it to Maaran as a token of gratitude.

We were starving and it was almost late evening. We drove to the small restaurant named Enfielders' Cafe in the nearby area. The restaurant was situated near a cliff and had a fantastic view. There were occasional lights from the villages nearby and the vehicles that went through the roads. It was -15 degrees Celsius and the hot food comforted us.

I looked at Maaran and said, 'Oru kadha solta, sir?' *(Sir, shall I tell you a story?)*

Maaran smirked at the reference I made from a popular Tamil movie, smiled and nodded.

Many months ago

In the bustling city where the rhythm of life beat synced to the sound of hurried footsteps, Gautham and Sundhari navigated their daily routines in the corporate world. Both worked tirelessly, their days filled with meetings, deadlines, and the constant white noise of their offices.

One evening, after particularly exhausting days at their respective offices, Gautham and Sundhari found themselves seeking solace in the familiar comfort of their favourite coffee shop at Varkala. The aroma of freshly ground beans enveloped them as they settled into a cosy corner, the soft glow of ambient lights casting a warm ambience overlooking the ocean, listening to the waves crashing the rocks down at the cliffs.

As they sipped their cocktails, the conversation turned to the mundane challenges of work, the pressures they faced, and the occasional victories that made the struggles worthwhile. While sharing stories and laughs, a moment of serendipity occurred. With a pinch of romance!

Gautham, keeping his glass strongly on the table, looked across at Sundhari and said, 'You know, sometimes I wish we could surprise each other just like we used to when we were kids. It feels like we've lost a bit of that magic in our hectic adult lives.'

Sundhari nodded, understanding the sentiment all too well. 'That's the honesty I never was expecting you to say. But yeah, I miss that spontaneity too. I miss surprising you! Maybe one day, love! What happened to that apartment you were looking for?'

Gautham — 'Okay, here's a surprise for you. I fixed one!'

In that shared moment of twinkling and longing for spontaneity, an idea sparked simultaneously in their minds. The weariness of the day seemed to lift, replaced by a renewed energy.

'I have an idea,' Gautham said, a mischievous grin on his face. 'Let's surprise each other tonight, just like the old times. Something to remind us that there's still room for magic in our busy lives.'

Sundhari smiled, her eyes lighting up with enthusiasm. They agreed to meet later that evening, each armed with a surprise for the other.

As the night fell and the city lights shimmered in the distance, Gautham and Sundhari met at a park, a quiet oasis amidst the urban chaos. The air was crisp, and the rustling leaves provided a soothing backdrop.

With a smile, they simultaneously revealed their surprises. Sundhari presented Gautham with a playlist of songs on a cassette and a handheld cassette player that held special meaning for them throughout the years. It was a musical journey through their friendship, a reminder that even in the busiest of times, the echoes of shared moments could be found in the simplest of things.

Gautham handed Sundhari a small, intricately wrapped package. She unwrapped it. There was a paper which read,

'Will you?' and a small, white-coloured film roll box was present. She opened it to find a key inside. As she took it in her hands, Gautham asked,

'Will you move in with me?'

Underneath the starlit sky, Gautham and Sundhari laughed, exchanged stories, and rediscovered the joy of surprise. In that tranquil moment, surrounded by the sea's heartbeats, they realized that no matter how demanding life became, the magic of spontaneity and the strength of their friendship would always endure, creating moments of warmth and connection amid the chaos of their busy lives.

Gautham was quite scared when he was about to ask her to move in with him in that apartment. Little did they know it gave them so many memories; good or bad or consoling or exciting.

'I was a little terrified if you would say no. I did not expect any answer from your side but what made you say — Yes?'

Back in the Enfielder's Cafe

Venba asked, 'Well, what did she say? What made her say yes to you?'

I said, 'Well, she said yes to me becau....'

A voice from near the terrace area entrance, 'Because it's worth it!'

I swiftly turned my head and there it was, a scene worth looking at.

'Hi, Gautham!'

My fluttering lips uttered, 'Sundhari!'

I stood up and ran to her. While we hugged tightly, it seemed as if she was almost breaking my ribs. 'I'm sorry, kannamma! I love you and I miss you so much.'

My other folks walked inside the cafe.

As I looked at her, with our hands still entangling each other, she came closer to my face and said, 'You are the artwork I can never get tired of!'

We walked towards the ledge and looked over the valley, standing so close to each other that we couldn't move any closer. She playfully knocked me head to head. Standing there, breathing peace, wiping tears, and sharing all the memories I encompassed these days — she was listening. I told her — 'I know that I should have communicated properly. I am so sorry that I have done this to you. And you still came for me. I dunno how to repay all this, Sundhari!'

Sundhari softly pinched my cheeks and said, 'Next time, say it to my face. Okay? And you are not a burden to anyone.'

I was still confused about her sudden appearance in Kashmir, so I asked — 'What made you travel this far?'

'You! Asshole!' She said as she held my jaws almost trying to break it off, and pulled me close to kiss. That was the longest kiss I ever had.

A bright-deep voice from behind, 'Hello traveller!'

I exclaimed, 'Hey Charlie! You came back. How did you know we... uh! You are the one who brought Sundhari here!'

'Yep!'

'And you're of friend of Manimaaran as well!'

'Yep!'

'You coordinated this whole thing with the other folks?'

'Yep!'

'And the guy who dropped you in his bike near the highway just for you to hitchhike with us was Maara too?'

'Yep!'

Seeing my mind getting blown away, Sundhari laughed along with Charlie and he gave her a high-five. The door opened and Priya walked in with Ravi.

Priya came and greeted Sundhari and they started talking.

'Venba should meet her!' I stormed into the cafe calling out to her. She should have been standing outside but maybe I missed her. Damn! I'm blind.

'VENBΛ!'

I looked at Priya and asked, 'Where is she? After all this drama, where has she gone?'

Charlie smirked at me, put his hand on my shoulder and said,' She wanted me to tell you that she was grateful to have spent time with you!'

Ravi seemed dull and he patted my back as he walked inside the cafe.

My voice was shrill, high, and crackling with cold and grief, 'Where's Maaran?'

Priya — 'He's taking Venba on a trip.'

I looked at Sundhari while she shook her head and I began to tear up badly.

I squealed, 'I didn't even get to say goodbye' and bawled very badly.

Venba from behind, 'Then say now!'

I turned around and hugged her. I cried and she consoled me while I saw others having tears in their eyes. Charlie's laughter filled the void. Clapping slowly, he walked outside.

'Do you have to go, Venba? Stay!'

'Sundhari has come a long way from home. Be with her! I'll be right back.'

Priya and Ravi joined the hug now. Ravi said, 'When you want to, just call us Venba! We will be there. Wherever you want us to be.'

She chuckled, 'Yeah, that's a fabulous idea, Ravi! And Thank you guys!'

Episode #16
SIXTEEN minutes

C*ontinued.... Some months later*

At Sundhari-Gautham's apartment

Morning Alarm rang

Sundhari switched off her alarm, woke up and turned to see that Gautham was already up early. 'Of course, he is a morning person!' she said as she walked into the bathroom.

She came out and went to the hall. It was empty and she checked the kitchen. It was squeaky clean too.

'Baby?' she called out to him.

She ran and checked in his room too — 'Gautham! Are you in here?' and she knocked on his bathroom door.

'Gautham! Where have you gone? This is the third time you're freaking me out so much. GAUTHAM!'

Walking back to the hall and peeking at the balcony, she saw his mobile phone near the TV.

'Gaut..'

And there he was, sitting on the balcony in a bean bag sipping hot tea.

'Babyyyy!' he said and raised his tea mug. He kept it on the small table nearby, jogged towards her, hugged her and said — 'Good morning, my love!'

She sunk into him — 'Budhdhu! You scare me a lot ra.'

'I love you, kannama!'

'I love you, Gautham!'

He sighed and she replied, 'I can hear your heartbeat, baby!' and looked into his eyes while she still hugged him. Gautham was almost breathing onto her face. She gently blew air to his face as he closed his eyes with a smile.

Sundhari — 'Your breath smells amazing.'

Opening his eyes, they started to kiss. He held her by her hips while she kept one hand on his shoulder and the other on his cheek. The soft moment lasted for a minute.

Slowly they walked towards the sofa and she pushed him onto it. She sat on his legs, tied her hair in a bun, and pulled him towards her by his t-shirt and again they started kissing but now it was louder.

She started to grab him by his hair and pulled on it quite forcibly, letting their tongues play with each other. She smiled while kissing him and removed his beige t-shirt. Caressing his back muscles at first, she began scratching using her nails.

Gautham commented 'Never can I convince you to cut your nails' for which she scratched more.

Gautham moaned and helped her remove her shirt. Passionately making out and biting each other, she gave him a hickey on the neck. He began to kiss Sundhari's weak spots while she kept pushing him away.

Gautham asked while she was breathing heavily, 'Wait, are you not comfortable?'

She guided her finger around his face and swiftly but gently grabbed his neck and said, 'Don't stop doing it!' and he continued.

The floor seems to be collecting one cloth after the other from the hot and engaging couple. The sofa was seeing too much action between them.

Gautham seemed to be louder than her today. She had to close his mouth with her hands and they shared a laugh in that intimate moment. In an intense moment, they happened to share an eye-contact when Sundhari said to him, 'Enough niceness Mr. Nice!'

The house got louder now, the sofa almost moving along with their movements, Sundhari felt the most high at a point.

Sundhari tapped on his shoulders and he stopped, while again he asked, 'Are you okay?'

Sundhari bit her teeth and replied with a tad bit of anger - 'Finish what we started!'

Gautham said to her, 'Baby! I love you' holding her face. And resumed.

Many passionate and intimate minutes later, they were sitting on the sofa, while Sundhari was sitting close to him, head on his chest and watching TV.

Sundhari tapped his head, 'Good boy! You have improved. Technically we both have improved!' saying, she wore his shirt.

He laughed.

'Kanna! I know I'm asking this question for the umpteenth time. What made you choose me - a random stranger you asked to sit with you for lunch at the mall?'

Clearing his throat and pretending to do it again with a smile, he spoke. 'Kannama! Since you are with me, it feels so special and very ordinary at the same time. I say ordinary because it feels very easy with you. Efforts don't seem huge. And I am not the person who remembers much about the dates, or days. But I remember so many tiny details between us, like the times we spent simple moments together, the times we fought or shared laughs and how we got along after that. The times your gestures made me laugh out loud but it was so practical and simple. You were another person like me, except that you were less anxious about stuff, less overthinking and more wonderful human. You! Are my home!'

'Gautham, your heart is beating so fast! So much for doing something for sixteen minutes.'

Gautham sniffled and asked her, caressing her hair — 'Tea venuma?' *(Do you want tea?)*

She replied, 'Nee venum!' *(I want you)*

He giggled, 'Hehehe! Alright! Get up! Let's take a bath and come. I'll make omelettes for us.'

Sundhari - 'Hey wait!' and pulled his left hand holding by his wrist.

She continued, 'What if...a baby happens between us?'

He sniffled and replied without a second thought, 'I mean, we both are not sure about raising a baby right now. But IF it happens, then I guess we face the music.'

Sundhari — 'You learnt to speak well. Go bring me tea! Then we can go take a bath. Overachiever!'

'At your service, my queen!' and he walked away saying, 'And no takebacks on the overachiever thing, okay!'

He brought two cups of tea and she said, 'Thanks to me, you became a tea addict.'

As she was checking her phone while drinking tea, she noticed an email from MakeMyTrip.

Sundhari — 'If you have to be more discreet about surprises. Be smarter!'

Gautham — 'What surprise?'

Sundhari — 'Here! See this.'

Checking the email she showed, he was surprised to find that it was air tickets from Trivandrum to Jaisalmer via Mumbai.

Mumbling at the ticket at first glance, Gautham spoke, 'Kannama! Did you book the tickets? I didn't do it. I swear.'

Gautham's phone rang from a new number.

'Hello! Gautham here.'

Episode #17
Epilogue

A few seconds later he continued, 'Priya! How are you? Wait, lemme put you on speaker.'

Priya — 'Hey Gautham! Okay, I wanted to ask you if you had booked me tickets to Jaisalmer.'

Sundhari said, 'Priya, hi! So, you also got it?'

Gautham said that he would connect Ravi on the Conference line.

After ringing for so long, he picked up and yawned loudly before he said Hello!

Ravi said in a hoarse voice — 'Hey bro! Wassup.'

'Wait!' and Gautham connected him to Priya via conference.

Gautham — 'Ravi! Priya is also on the line. Sundhari is nearby. We got tickets via email from Makemytrip to Jaisalmer. Do you know anything about it?'

Ravi — 'Aah! My brain is still upside down. Well, Jaisalmer! This is going to be nostalgic. See you all at the dunes. I booked them last night. Get ready! 2 more weeks. No questions asked!'

And he cut the call immediately.

Priya — 'Okay, what was that?'

Sundhari asked the right question — 'Should we ask Maaran about this?'

Gautham — 'Nah! He will be in Nepal now. He called me over the phone last week. Okay, I'll call you back in some time, Priya.'

Sundhari's phone pinged with a new message. It was a video from an unknown number with a pamphlet about the tent stay in Jaisalmer near the desert.

She downloaded it and said, 'These ads and promotions are getting outrageous da. Cha! We just spoke about it and now I have an ad on WhatsApp..... Wait, no!'

And while she clicked play, Charlie was in the frame setting up the frame. It was in the backdrop of the desert in Jaisalmer. He moved the phone towards the tent. Charlie started talking.

'Hey! I know you are so confused right now. I'd let the person responsible to speak.'

A woman appeared wearing cargo, a black tee and a oversized white shirt, a scarf around her neck, and a big fedora hat hiding her face. She removed the hat and sunglasses.

'Hey, guys! It's me, Venba. Yeah! If you are seeing this, it's been a long time since I shot this. I don't wish to say when! They stopped chemo last week. I asked Charlie to take me here. It was my wish to him that you guys travel one more time with a well-planned schedule. Meet new people! Love deeply!'

Her voice was a bit raspy. Venba was looking tired and weak and probably looked like a different person. Her cancer got worse and the chemo sessions took the health out of her. But not her will and the joy she had with us. The last time they saw her was in Kashmir at that Enfielder's Cafe restaurant. Venba continued,

'Each of you means the world to me. I can't express how much your support has meant, especially during the toughest times. I know I left you guys when I needed someone to be with me. It's okay, life happens. Nah! That's bullshit. I was adamant, I guess. It's a very old habit I picked up from my friend Gautham. I...uh...It's very bright! I need my sunglasses, it's too bright!

I wanted to thank each one of you individually and personally for being there, but time might not permit it. Your stories have

been my pillars, my confidants, and my source of strength. Without you, I don't think I could have faced the challenges that life threw my way.

Gautham! Sundhari! I hope you folks are doing fine. I love you guys! And Gautham, I hope you are getting help as needed.

Ravi! You have become the fittest among us. I'm glad you quit alcohol and started to become a hot version of yourself. And Priya! You are like the daughter I never had. It's not technically possible to have such an older daughter for my age. But you get what I'm saying. I was glad we met during the Valley of Flowers trek and thank you for taking me to Hemkund Sahib.

My friends! I need you all to know that this may or may not be my last video. I'm at a crossroads, and I don't know what lies ahead. Life has a mysterious way of unfolding, and as much as I wish I could predict the future, I can't. My test results will be back soon and I'm ready to see whether the cancer caught me well or has gone for good. But please, hold onto the memories we've shared. Cherish everything that made us feel alive. Gautham, I know you're fond of writing letters. I thought of writing one for each of you too. But a video felt more personal, man.

I have booked these tents for you guys much in advance. Ravi would take care of the plan as he promised to me. I wish to be here with you all but I cannot promise you anything. You guys find out when you come here.

Charlie interrupted from behind the camera — *'Here meaning? These tents or after this life?'*

Venba smirked, *'I can't say, Charlie! You of all should know that.'*

Charlie replied, *'Well, I was asking questions on their behalf.'*

She smiled - *'We will see.'*

As she uttered those words, a gust of wind tossed her phone to the ground. Startled, Venba put up the phone again, her face smiling through everything. The mystery of her living hung in the air to these friends like an unspoken secret.

'To my dearest friends, I love you more than words can convey. Thank you for being my light in the darkness. Take care, live high and if you can, just remember me with love. See ya!'

With that, Venba shed tears uncontrollably and abruptly ended the recording, her emotions pouring into every word.

Sundhari was sitting there with tears in her eyes and cheeks. Gautham was struck, couldn't say a word and his left eye shed a drop of tear.

'Kannama!' he said and she stood up to hold his hand. He continued,

'Is she?'

'Venba is a woman of mystery. She beats me in that aspect. We don't know about her test results yet. Let's go to the desert and find out. I want to fulfil her wish. And not do any detective work around this mystery.'

Gautham's phone lit up. It was a message from Priya.

It read,

'Let's go. Let's go and meet, Venba!'

And their journey began!

Thank you for reading this story with me! I hope you keep supporting me in this journey. Venba was a butterfly in each of their lives. The butterfly effect proved to be real for them. Perspectives were changed.

And now you ask yourself, who is your butterfly effect? :)